Charles Pelham Mulvany, Amos Henry Chandler

Lyrics, Songs and sSonnets

By Amos Henry Chandler and Charles Pelham Mulvany

Charles Pelham Mulvany, Amos Henry Chandler

Lyrics, Songs and sSonnets
By Amos Henry Chandler and Charles Pelham Mulvany

ISBN/EAN: 9783744766623

Printed in Europe, USA, Canada, Australia, Japan

Cover: Foto ©Andreas Hilbeck / pixelio.de

More available books at **www.hansebooks.com**

LYRICS,

SONGS AND SONNETS.

BY

AMOS HENRY CHANDLER

AND

CHARLES PELHAM MULVANY.

Toronto:

HUNTER, ROSE & CO.

MDCCCLXXX.

PREFACE.

WE lay before the Canadian literary public this volume of verse, the work of two Canadian writers. The object of the Poems on Religious Subjects herein published is to assert the claims of religious thought from the liberal standpoint. Some of the lyrics by both writers have had the advantage of appearing in our *Canadian Monthly and National Review,* which has done so much to foster a native literature under the editorship of Mr. G. Mercer Adam. Some of the lyrics, relating to classical history, and the Latin poems, have been honoured with a place in *Kottabos,* the serial representing the University of Dublin.

AMOS HENRY CHANDLER,
New Brunswick.

CHARLES PELHAM MULVANY,
Toronto.

MAY, 1880.

LIBRUM SUUM DEDICANT

CIVES DUO,

Tibi Goldwin Smith,

STRENUO

LIBERTATIS VINDICATORI.

TO LIBERTY.

Lo! toward the West a swift-descending light,
That soon shall circle the long clouded earth,
Wide blazing, as a gem of priceless worth,
Those beams shall yet pierce through the darkest
night
Of ignorance and sin, with flashes bright;—
Dispel the fogs, as doth the glowing birth
Of summer's sun, the mists, when song and mirth
The East vales gladden: still pursue thy flight.

Shine steady on, O Star of Liberty!
Till warring sects and superstitious creeds
No longer bind the consciences of men;
Till shackles fall, and every slave is free;
Till bread, not stone, is sent to crying needs—
The world shall hail thee her deliverer, then!

A. H. C.

March 4th, 1880.

LYRICS OF HISTORY AND LIFE.

BY

CHARLES PELHAM MULVANY.

Ce petit livre, O ma chère,
Que Monsieur Rose a publié ;
C'est le tombeau, c'est la parterre,
Où ma jeunesse est enterrée.

LYRICS OF HISTORY AND LIFE.

STELLA.

" ONLY a woman's hair ! "
Found as such relics are found
After long years, when the night
Closed on what once had been Swift,—
Stella's the raven-black tress,—
Swift's the inscription, no doubt.

Whereat reporters and critics
Cast in their Liliput minds
What the dead giant might mean,
Was it the misathrophe's scorn
Mocking himself in his pain,
Making the love that had died
Point one last epigram more ?

Not so, reporters and critics !
Read how, the night that she died,

Swift sat alone in the dark,
Tearless, unable to think ;—
No ! in these words are the tears',
And the thoughts that would come not that day.

" Only a woman's hair ! "
All that was left of her now,
All that was left of a love
True through the world, through the years—
Born with his boyhood, to share
Battle and darkness and need,
Linking his youth to old age—
Proud when the Victor prevailed,—
Glad when the athlete was crowned,—
True when the dark hours came on,—
Smiling to calm the wild eyes,—
Kissing the lips fierce with scorn.

" Only a woman's hair ! "
How he remembered when first
Seen as it curled over eyes
Bent on his own, as they two,
Under the formal, close-trimmed,
High-Dutch, dwarf trees of Moor Park,—
Types of the pedant its lord,—
Learned a new language of soul—
Breathed a new life that set free
Genius and Youth, Hope and Love.

" Only a woman's hair ! "
And he had seen it so often
Blown by the Laracor winds,—
Brightened by suns that have set
Where the stream shewed—does it shew
Still,—the grey Parsonage walls ;
Still those grey walls which that guest
Coming and going made glad—
Graced with the charm of her youth, .
Laughter from merriest lips !
Bright light from kindliest eyes !

" Only a woman's hair ! "
Looked at so often alone,
After the feverish day,
When amid mean men called great,
He, with the sword of his wit,
Smote ;—and that dark tress recalled
Home and her, far over seas !
Looked at even then as he wrote
" Journals to Stella" each day—
Each thought of his, each hope, hers—
Soothed with pet names like a child ;
Never was true love more true—
Never were tenderer words !

' Only a woman's hair ! "
Here in this house, home no more !

Here where the garden-walks wind
Under the barbarous, grim,
Gothic Cathedral's grey towers—
Here where the bold words were written,
Calling the slaves to be free,
And in dead Ireland's name
Fronting defiant her foes—
Then when his Dublin rose round him,
Guarding "the Dean," till the foe
Felt his fierce scorn and was foiled.
Dear to his country and her—
Was it not well with him then ?

Only a woman's hair !"
Not of Vanessa but Hers—
Not of the meteor that beaming
Bright in a frivolous hour,
Passed to its place in the darkness,
Leaving remorse and dismay ;
But of his Star, that still shone,
Then when all else was eclipsed,—
Genius and Manhood and Wit,
Friendship of statesmen and peers,—
Leaving that wreck of a life
Only the love of the poor—
Only his country's regret—
" Only a woman's hair !"

Ireland ! if yet in the years
Being made free, thou shalt think
Then of those great ones thy sons,—
Building the marble to Swift,
Wilt thou not also to Stella
Build in that day ?—to his Star—
Star of that great stormy life—
Star that still shines where he feels
" Fierce indignation" no more !

POPPÆA.

No. 1.—At the Theatre.

DARK tresses made rich with all treasures,
　　Earth's gold-dust, and pearls of the sea—
She is splendid as Rome that was Cæsar's,
　　And cruel as Rome that was free !

Could I paint her but once as I found her,
　　From her porphyry couch let her lean,
With the reek of the circus around her—
　　Who is centre and soul of the scene :

Grey eyes that glance keen as the eagle
　　When he swoops to his prey from on high;

Bold arms by the red gold made regal—
  White breast, never vexed with a sigh:

And haughty her mien as of any
  Her sires whom the foemen knew well,
As they rode through the grey mist at Cannæ,
  Ere consul with consular fell.

Unabashed in her beauty of figure—
  Heavy limbs and thick tresses uncurled
To our gaze, give the grace and the vigour
  Of the race that has conquered the world.

And fierce with the blood of the heroes
  In their sins and their virtues sublime—
Sits the Queen of the world that is Nero's,
  And as keen for a kiss or a crime!

But the game that amuses her leisure
  Loses zest as the weaker gives way—
And the victor looks up for her pleasure
  Shall he spare with the sword point or slay?

Half-grieving she gathers her tresses,
  Now the hour for the games has gone by,
And those soft arms, so sweet for caresses,
  Point prone, as she signs, "let him die!"

No. 2.—In Nero's Gardens. A.D. 67.

By Pollux! no time to wait, for the gathering crowds
    are rolled
From Phaon's ivory gate to Cæsar's House of Gold!
For to-night a new delight, new pleasures the good
    gods send
If away from the Feast to-night, thou art not Cæsar's
    friend.
From forum and temple gates behold how the torches
    rise,
Fair as the Emperor's fates and bright as are Acte's
    eyes!
Gay with shouting and song are the wide illumined
    ways,—
Each house to the passing throng a festival wreath
    displays.
From the Esquiline and the camp they are flocking
    by Tiber's side;
Sublime with many a lamp Suburra lights on the tide.
No room for the laggard who waits, so fast the crowds
    are whirled
To Poppæa's garden gates, where Cæsar shall feast
    the world.

The gods give us stars for light, but Cæsar, a god
    below,
Giving us day for night, bids all to the banquet go,—

Spread in the gardens fair, where the stately gates
    stand wide,
And for all is room and to spare, and never was
    guest denied.
Virtue is welcome and vice, each class-distinction
    that springs
From old-world notions too nice for the stage when
    CÆSAR sings!
Patrician ladies in state, on the necks of slaves up-
    borne,
And brides of the Arch, who wait where bride-veil
    never was worn!
All Rome's pride and her pests, her glory and greed
    and shame,
To-night shall be CÆSAR'S guests, "Circenses and
    bread" may claim.

Never were seen such sights as the Emperor's gardens
    show!
All the world's delights out-spread wherever you go;
Tables are there for all, and couches for whoso will,
Slave girls come at your call, and the cooks have a
    royal skill;
Bakers that roast and knead, and cunning women
    that toil,
Mixing fresh poppy seed, sweet honey and faultless
    oil—

Fish from the Lucrine track, and boar from Umbria's
plains,
Skylark's tongues no lack, and store of nightingale s
brains—
And of all wines men know, whose cost is beyond
compare,
Flowing in streams below, or fountain-tost in the
air ;
Or sailed on in mimic seas by vessels of pearl that
hold
Pilots who give to the breeze their tresses and zones
of gold.

The gods give us stars for light, but CÆSAR, a god
below,
With lamps that are living to-night illumines the
goodly show ;
Lo ! where in order meet, like statues on either hand,
Ranged in a fiery street, the torches of CÆSAR
stand ;
Each made firm in his place to a pillar of steel,
throat-fast,
Pitch-smeared from foot-sole to face, like a shape in
bitumen cast—
So the imperial might let Rome and the world discern,
Greeting his gods to-night, such torches shall CÆSAR
burn.

Lo, where he comes ! behold the flush of the chariot
race
Under the diadem's gold on the cruel, beautiful
face,
Crowned with rose and with bay, and watching in
god-like scorn
The flight of the flames that play on the path of the
purple-born !
At his side the slave of slaves that rules earth's Lord
for a day,
Spurning like Venus the waves of her foot-ward-fallen
array,
With lovely, large eyes, whose dream, far-thoughted
of new desires,
Heeds little the shapes that scream and writhe from
a thousand fires.

No. 3.—The Death of Nero.

Strew flowers for Rome's last Roman prince, as we
cry with bated breath,
To the queen, Rome's mother and goddess, our Lady
of Love and death;
For the great house born of Venus, her gift to Rome
in vain—
Since the last, like the first of the Cæsars, by treason of Rome lies slain !

"What owest thou, Rome, to the Neros?" Let the
   Punic shades avow
That the greed of the base Pretorian has avenged
   Metaurus now.
Lost age that we deemed the golden; when Beauty
   and Love took flower,
And Art, like a new Apollo, seemed throned in world-
   wide power!
Did he sin with caprice colossal? at his lust grew
   nations pale?
On what else but the world's arena could the Venus-
   born prevail?
With a sway that earth has seen not and never shall
   see again,
Unsated with love of women, unsparing in blood of
   men.

That night the Prince lay rose-crowned, imperial, a
   god to behold!
The setine sparkling beside him in crystal of priceless mould,
Well-wrought and carved with the image of Aphrodite divine,
Her fair limbs naked and glowing through amber
   waves of the wine;
And with hands that threw down the sceptre he
   tuned the more welcome lyre

To its wildest notes, as he sang of Troy overthrown
    by fire—
How of old to the Son of Venus the spectre at mid-
    night came,
And the ill news brought of treason wrought, and
    city wrapt in flame.
Trembled and thrilled the lyre notes we had heard
    and remembered well—
Over Rome flaming round us that prelude and chorus
    swell !
But sudden ceased the music its strain of ill-omened
    name,
When pale as the ghost it sang of, the slave with ill-
    tidings came :
" Galba revolts—the legions march from Spain and
    the Gauls !"
Untasted from ghastly lips the priceless crystal falls !
The city risen in tumult, the palace gates beset,
To set a price on his head, the servile senate are met.

We fly through the gathering darkness, whose only
    hope is in flight,
To a villa, his gift to Phaon, by aid of Venus and night.
There with what thoughts we waited ! saw night and
    morning change,
From joy cast down so sudden, our new despair
    seemed strange ;

When, hark to the sound of horse hoofs! the pur-
suers are here at last,—
With the sword we give thee, CÆSAR, thou canst not
strike home too fast!
They came on us, the traitors!—but all was over now,
And the dews of death had gathered on the pale,
imperial brow;
They tried to staunch the wound in vain, the lips
faint smiling said,
"Is this then your fidelity?" The soul of NERO
sped.

MESSALINA.

The object of this "dramatic lyric" is not to white-wash "the
wickedest Empress," but to plead for the truth that "there is a soul
of good in things evil." We have our very highly coloured picture of
Messalina from Tacitus, and from the sixth satire of Juvenal, both
writers avowedly hostile to the Cæsars. Juvenal, born like Saint
Thomas, at Aquinum, was as dogmatic in his vituperation as the
Saint of the middle ages. Messalina could not have been utterly bad,
for during the few days between her detection and death, she was
protected not only by her mother, but by the Chief of the Vestal
Virgins. And Tacitus relates that, years after her death, she had
friends who took the part of her son Britanicus.

"Two sides to a story"! one of mine
Points the lash of each poisoned line
In the famed Sixth Satire, our sex's shame—
Pilloried in MESSALINA'S name—

Smooth flows the verse, and the angry muse,
Rich in the rhetoric of the stews,
Lingers each phase of vice to tell,
Loving the task of libel well.

Who knows not the picture AQUINAS paints?
I mean the Satirist's not the Saint's—
The Palace left at the midnight hour,
The orgie in lewd Lysisca's bower—
Whose reckless revels the breasts behold
That bore Britanicus, decked with gold;
The foul life's licence of lust and wine—
His tale which the world has heard—hear *mine*.

I was no Empress, not mine the praise,
" Born in the purple " of Rome's last days—
To cringe to eunuch and slave, and fret
In a prison of courtly etiquette—
But a Roman woman, whose grandsire died,
As he fought and revelled, at Sulla's side—
Not more his heiress in name and land
Than in passionate heart and strong right hand:

In strength of the ancient Roman stamp,
That swam the Tiber from Tarquin's camp;
Perhaps in courage to match that one
Who saved the city, and doomed her son!
Or her's who wept not her jewels twain,
Lavished and lost for Rome in vain!

Unmoved in her love's imperial pride,
When Freedom perished and Gracchus died.

Or well content with a calmer life—
The sweet home-ways of the Roman wife—
To spin her wool by the household fire,
While her boys are piling the pine blaze higher !
At the hour of rest when the day fulfils,
And the sun is low on the Sabine hills,
Such hours, such scenes, our Rome had then
For the mothers and mates of her bravest men.

Even I—had it pleased the gods above—
The sort of woman that good men love !
Good to be joined as gold with gold,
Pure with the pure and brave with bold—
Proud of the heart whose worth she knew,
Giving in pledge of true love, true ;
For Love worth love, be sure my own
With mutual fires as bright had shone.

What sort of hero was mine for mate ?
What kind of Cæsar bestowed by Fate ?
Bold with grammarians war to wage—
Skilled in the lore of Numa's age—
With whom both folly and cowardice came—
A double curse to the Claudian name,
Yet worse to me, whom ill Fortune gave
To a freedman's client, a eunuch's slave !

Small joy had I in my place of pride,
Though to empire wed as the world is wide ;
Though when I passed to my service vowed,
Thirty legions their eagles bowed.
I could not bear it, reaction came,—
Wild quest of pleasure that knows not shame,—
Such passion-madness as, ere the end,
To those they ruin, the good gods send.

For the gods ordain since earth began,
By perfect conditions the perfect man—
Vice comes or virtue, good comes or sin,
From the world without to the world within ;
Life's *form* may vary, *itself* the same,
Cornelia's love—Messalina's shame,
Through all whose passion, condemn who will,
Some voice of womanhood pleadeth still !

EPICHARIS.

Tacitus relates the heroic death of Epicharis, who was concerned in the last conspiracy against Nero, and on the failure of the plot was put to the severest torture by the tyrant, in hopes, as Tacitus says, that so delicate a frame, accustomed to the most voluptuous life, could not bear the pain of the rack prolonged over three days.

HER silk-wrought robes with gold bedight,
From loving eyes scarce hid from sight
Her body shaped for love's delight—

Her life seemed only made for this,—
For song and sleep, for cup and kiss,—
Love's slave and Queen, EPICHARIS.

Yet they, the last of Roman men
Who banded for Rome's freedom then,
Their cause confided to her ken.

The plotters failed, but Nero tried
That she who knew them; torture-plied,
Should tell of each tyrannicide.

Two days upon the rack she bore
The pangs that ever pressed her more,
Yet still was silent as before.

From prison borne upon the third,
She feared that agony deferred
Might wring out an unwilling word.

She said, " Ye happy Powers Divine,
Who punish poor, weak loves like mine,
Unused to prayer at any shrine ;

" My first, last prayer I pray to ye ?
Whatever Gods above may be,
This soul enslaved, may death set free

B

" From love, from life, to seek the deep
Repose of that enduring sleep—
Let that long night my secret keep.

" So shall the safe grave hide away
This poor, soiled life, that shames the day,
Her's that could Sin, but not Betray."

Some fragment of her prison chain
Around her neck she wrought to strain,
And so the martyr lay self-slain.

A slave set free by Death alone,
Who owned no altar, feared no throne,
And with scant prayer to gods unknown.

Yet in the stately sentence sage
Of Tacitus, the ennobling page
Shall bear her name from age to age.

So let him read, whose wisdom will,
The germ of Truth in Error still,—
The soul of Good in all things ill.

WHY THE DEVIL REFUSED ABSOLUTION.

See "St. Martin of Tours, surnamed the Miracle Worker."—*Bollandist Lives of the Saints.*

ST. MARTIN of Tours was weary outright,
He had preached all day, he had prayed all night,
With a scourge to his back, with hair-cloth to his
    skin,
He had fasted since dawn from all but sin ;
He had exorcised the possessed that lay
Writhing and foaming in his way ;
He had cleansed the body and shrived the soul
Of the loathsome lazars his kiss made whole.

But sad was Martin of Tours, in spite
Of penance by day and prayer by night,
And hopeless grown of his power to win
In the deadly struggle with deadly sin—
For the fiends returned that he scared away,
And night made foul what he cleansed by day.
And the miracle worker in vain made whole
The loathsome body and leprous soul.

So the Saint exclaimed, " Since my work began
I have prayed to God, I have preached to man,
With never a sign—for all I plead—
That Heaven will hear or earth will heed ;

I sing my Mass, but the fresh flower-bloom
Of sin is more sweet than the incense-fume.
I point to Heaven's Queen in vain—to her,
Earth's Queen of Beauty mankind prefer.

And I call to thee in the darkness, owned
Supreme of sin upon earth enthroned,
And I name thy name in my heart's despair
Of impotent faith and unanswered prayer—
Who, from Best corrupted, art now the Worst—
From fairest angel made fiend most curst—
Whose devil's caldron is seething still
With the world-wide ferment of human ill:

With war's perdition, with peace made sure
For coward commerce to cheat the poor—
With the creed's shrill curses, the church's lust
For the sword she cankers with blood-red rust;
With nations starving ere quite the pitch
Of their cry of hunger can rouse the rich—
With the landlord's fat purse that famine fills—
With all hate that maddens, all love that kills.

And, I say to thee, Satan, peace! be still!
Leave the world and the flesh to their wicked will,
With no Devil to play on their hopes and fears
By his cursed craft of four thousand years.

For alas ! though the Serpent's voice be mute,
Bright eyes will covet forbidden fruit,
And hearts put faith in the primal lie,
Though no fiend whisper, 'Thou shalt not die.'

And I dare to forgive thee in the name
Of Him, who, first to confront thee came,
Proclaiming, while this lost earth He trod,
That the Son of Man is the Son of God;
Through all the ages of storm and strife,
Who walks the waters of human life—
In the name of the Sinless, to Sin I say,
Repent thee, cease, be absolved this day."

He spake ! Stood there shape the good Saint by ?—
Was there voice or any that made reply ?—
The unrobed girl-demon with gold-bright hair,
Who haunted the hermit's desert lair—
Or he—the last fiend the dark ages knew,
Who fled from the ink-horn that Luther threw ;
Or the cold, keen scoffer of modern mien,
So late by a greater than Luther seen ?

I know not.   It may be there came a strain—
The unconscious voice of the good man's brain,
" No word of pity or prayer can reach
The power called evil thou dost beseech,

Since Force and Matter the world that frame,
Are good or evil, but as a name—
And sin's forgiveness and sin's control
Can but be sought in the human soul."

THEODORA.   A. D. 540.

" The Empress Theodora showed either the most cynical indiffer-
ence to the public opinion, which she thus reminded of her own early
career, or the loftiest insensibility to vulgar fear.   : . .   She who
had been the miserable victim of the passions of man was the first
to build a Refuge for Fallen Women."--*History of the Emperor
Justinian.*

SHE built neither palace nor church,
She gave not to Cæsar or God,
In pride, or devotion, her wealth ;
Not her's is the fresco we see
In Ravenna's Basilica still,
Fair-wrought in the azure and gold,
The face and the form, at New Rome,
Love's slave and love's empress, by love
Made bare and abased to all shame,
By Love clad with purple and crowned !

" I have willed it," she said ; " let my walls
By the blue waves of Helle, rise fair

As the cypress, and firm as the hills
Let them stand and endure—while there flows
Through the streets of the city life's tide—
While the noise of man's riotous lust,
Man's waste of soul, body, and brain,
Makes its brute cry of selfishness heard !
Man's victim and slave through all time,
Herein shall seek refuge and find !

" From the streets, that in glare or in gloom,
Like a stepmother cruel and hard,
Lead the way to no home but the gates
Of Hades—from garden and hall,
Made fair for forbidden fruit !
From the palace where Wealth has his will,
And only the marble is pure,
To the dark arch where, passing, one sees,
Through the dingy red curtain, how vice
Is naked—and is not ashamed.

" From Eros, named Anteros now—
From Her who was Venus, and is
Libitina ; death's goddess, not Love's !
Who blights youth's best bloom, and makes void
All hearts with the curse of her kiss.
When the sweetness is past, and the pain
Of the withered ones, strewn to the winds,
Grows fierce at the envied green leaves !

In Passion's dark hour of regret
For the kisses so longed for, yet loathed.

" I have known it—have drained to the lees
That chalice of passion and pain!
Though undraped, undegraded, his bride   •
The imperial Candaules could claim,
Whose " Gyges" was Rome, and the gaze
Of the Blue partisans and the Green,
By the vast amphitheatre hailed,
Till faction grew mute, and the meed
Of a beauty Imperial already
The nephew of Justin decreed.

" Theodora, who once in New Rome
Danced robeless as Pyrrha or Eve !
. Theodora, of empire who proved
Not wholly unworthy, whose word
' It were well to meet Death on the Throne !'
Gave new nerve to her panic-struck lord,
In the teeth of defeat and revolt;
Who swayed the Sixth Council, who forced
To sign her pet heresy's creed
The infallible Pontiff himself.

" Therefore I, Theodora, who stoop
To no shame of the men that I scorn--
Nor desire their good word, nor would seem
To be aught but the woman I am--

Build here, for the women, man's slaves,
And victims of man and of Fate,
Who are what I was, who am now
Crowned Empress of Rome and the world—
This Refuge and House of Retreat,
By margin of Helle's blue wave."

SARAH CURRAN. 1803.

" She is far from the land where her young hero sleeps."—MOORE.

YES ! far indeed, the happy, prosperous wife !
    All whose home-paths the home-grown blossoms
        strew—
Since needing rest, and woman-like, her life
    Forgot the old love and made choice anew.

Yes ! through all else, those unforgotten hours,
    Bright, less by sun than thunder storm, hold sway,
And through all solace of the home-grown flowers,
    Recall that nameless tomb-stone far away.

Through mists of Dublin fog, St. Michan's spire
    Guides where the waste of city grave-yard lies—
Where, 'mid the squalor of the Church-street mire,
    Of death's bastile the iron gratings rise.

In strange exemption from the taint of death,
  There incorrupt, John rests, and Henry Shears—
First in our land who sowed the dragon's teeth,
  Yet reaped not harvest of insurgent spears ;—

Red harvest ripe for glorious " Ninety-eight!"
  But there, low-leaning by the grey church wall,
That long, blank slab without a name or date,
  Marks where he sleeps, the youngest, best of all !

Can she recall those high hopes ere they fell,
  As fall earth's noblest, amid mean men spared—
Or grieve for the true heart she once knew well,
  Whose love for her was but with Freedom shared ?

High.hopes, how fallen—the deep-planned, sudden
  The broken ranks of Union re-enrolled— [blow—
The gathered arms that should confront the foe,
  And at its centre seize the tyrant's hold !—

One hour's base riot saw those high hopes quelled
  Saw foiled revolt made murder's countersign—
So falls by felon hands the green flag held—
  So Cato's cause, if served by Catiline !

Let the high aim the hasty deed redeem ;
  Such aims to-day the cause he loved might save
No more a faction's cry—a pauper's dream—
  Till then, lost hero ! keep thy nameless grave.

                    SACKVILLE, N. B., Jan. 26, 1880.

EMMA, LADY HAMILTON.

" Don't let poor Nelly starve."

THOSE thrilling moments before Nelson died,
Rocked to his long rest on the crimsoned wave,
While round him wept the bravest of the brave—
To his last words they listened eager-eyed,
As Hardy kissed the Hero : " ere the tide
Can change, prepare to anchor," so to save
The ships that day for England—then, " I leave
My Lady Hamilton my country's care."
What answer did those sacred words receive ?
Did England " do her duty" to the man
Whose world-famed signal fired Trafalgar's van?
How did the lost love of the hero fare ?
And can our prim morality believe
That God and man alike reject the prayer ?

ELINOR'S RETURN.

EARL Christian sailed upon the sea,
Dear to the blessed Saints was he ;

God's angels, with their wings of white,
Guarded him both in storm and fight.

For Christian's sword had dyed the flood,
As deep as hell, with heathen blood.

He slew the heathen, young and old,
And burned their towns, and took their gold.

God gave good gifts to Christian then,
A ship fleet-sailing, feared of men;

A woman loving, gentle, fair,
Of queenly beauty past compare,—

The lady Elinor, and three
Fair daughters to her lord bare she.

Three beds of gold the ladye made,
Those children there each night were laid.

And night and morn she took good heed
They had both ale and wine and mead.

" My lot is blessed above men;
What lack I yet ? " said Christian then.

That night his ship lay wrecked on shore,
That night died Ladye Elinor.

Bitter grief did Christian dree,
For that ship and that Ladye.

The women of the South are fair;
They have grey eyes and gold-bright hair;

And from the South a woman came,
Whose beauty shone on men like flame.

On her white breast she bound a spell
That made Earl Christian love her well.

She kissed Earl Christian tenderly,
That he might not hear his children cry ;

And she spake love-runes into his ear,
That he might forget those children dear.

Those three fair babes waxed thin and cold,
For she took away their beds of gold ;

And ever as grew they thin and pale,
Never she gave them bread or ale,

So that they cried to God full sore
For their dead mother, Elinor.

"Oh, would God give our mother back,
Good ale and bread we should not lack !

Oh, might our mother now behold,
We should not shiver in the cold."

That mother heard her children cry,
Far off with God, above the sky;

Who sent her soul from Heaven away,
To the graveyard where her body lay.

Oh woe was that poor ghost alone,
To lift that heavy churchyard stone !

She had no clothes but her coffin sheet,
And the watch-dogs barked at her passing feet !

She came when by Earl Christian's door,
Her eldest child sat weeping sore.

" My child, what dost thou here so late,
In wind and rain at thy father's gate ? "

" Thy child ! my mother's face was red,
But thine is pale as are the dead ;

My mother's robes were silk and gold,
But thine are dark with churchyard mould ! "

" Ah ! how can I be fair or red,
Who have so many a day been dead ?

Ah ! how can I wear silk or gold,
Who lie all day in churchyard mould ? "

The Ladye wept as she stood beside
The bed of Christian and his bride.

" Earl Christian you rest softly here,
While I lie cold on my death bier ;

Fair Ladye, you sleep warm in bed,
While my children lack both ale and bread.

Farewell, my eldest child, Christine,
Let gold, and ships, and land be thine.

Farewell my second child, Helen,
For you shall be well loved of men—

But thou my babe come home with me,
I would God's Mother should look on thee.

I go, but if I come again
An evil wierd I rede ye then!"

Glad rose the Earl with the morning red,
But his youngest child lay by him dead.

And folks have said, how, since that night,
That ghost was feared in the new wife's sight;

And whenever she heard the night dog's wail,
She gave those children wine and ale.

NEPTUNUS.

(Considerably altered from Heine.)

COLD falls the night on starless seas and skies,
Stretched on the waves the weary north wind lies,
With cracked and shrieking voice he shouts and sings
The maddest yarns about the maddest things,—

Storms, shipwrecks, flying Dutchman, all that be
The wicked, ghastly secrets of the sea,—
So wicked, that they make each water-sprite
Leap from the water, screaming for delight.

But lo! on the wet sands,
A stranger stands,—
About his manly form in many a fold,
A Spanish mantle wraps him from the cold ;
The storm blows wilder as he passes by,
And when he steps, red sparkles flash and fly :
He hastens on to where that lonely light
Shines from the fisher's cottage on the height.

Her father and brother are out at sea,—
The fisherman's daughter is there alone ;
No maiden half so fair as she
Can at market, or dance, or church be shown ;
And her merry gray eyes, and her gold-bright curls ,
Win the love of all men and the hate of all girls.
And now she sits by the fire alone,
And over her face, in the red fire-light,
The golden curls fall glossy and bright.

The stranger enters—how she flushes red !
" I come to keep my promise, as I said,—
I also come to tell to you my dear,
Good news that may astonish you to hear !

The good old times are come again,—
The grand old Pagan ages, when
The gods took wives of the daughters of men,
Begetting heroes, men of renown,
Who mightily ruled over castle and town,—
Lo ! now, come home, be queen and wife of mine,
For I am Neptune, Ruler of the Brine.

The fisher may search for his home and his daughter,
Nothing is there but the cold, gray water !
      And the men were sad,
      And women were glad,
That she never came back, however they sought her.

ALMANSOR.

(A variation considerably altered from Heine.)

At Cordova the cathedral hath a dome full fair to
    see,
Reared upon colossal columns, three score and ten
    and three ;

And on cupola and column, many a text and legend
    old
From the Koran wreaths in arabesque of azure hues
    and gold.

On those walls of Christian worship still the Moorish
  blazons glow,
Wrought by pious hands to Allah many centuries
  ago,—

Centuries old, yet fresh in beauty, still all uneffaced
  are they,
While in Time's unsparing torrent kings and creeds
  are swept away !

In the cloister at Cordova, at the vesper hour of
  prayer,
Stands Almansor ben Abdallah, with low voice he
  murmers there—

As he looks unto the pillars and the giant dome on
  high,
To the walls with gold emblazoned and with lapis
  lazuli :

" Oh, ye strong and giant pillars, oh, ye massive
  mighty walls,
Reared of old to Allah's worship, now the Christian's
  servile thralls,—

Where the Muzzin praised the Prophet in the olden
  faithful days—
Now the Priests are chanting Masses to the Christian Idol's praise—

Where the people prayed to Allah in the good time
    long ago,
Bells are ringing, incense steaming, all is puppet
    pomp and show.

You the strong, and ever-during, can submit that this
    shall be—
Not Time, and not the Christian Creed, but Love
    hath conquered me !"

By the gold-clad, lace-fringed Prelate o'er the Font
    Almansor leant,
His head bowed in graceful reverence, scornful smil-
    ing as he bent,

Quickly left he the cathedral—town and tower were
    far behind,
Till his hair blew wildly backward, and his plume
    streamed on the wind.

Riding fast along the valley, where the Guadalqui-
    ver flows,
And the snow-white almond blossoms, and the golden
    orange glows ;

But so wild a rider stays not for gold fruit or silver
    stream,
Till through woods of Alcolea, sees he castle win-
    dows gleam.

Soon in halls of Alcolea, twelve fair ladies lead the
    ball,
With twelve knights of highest honour, and Alman-
    sor chief of all.

In the halls of Alcolea now the festal sound has
    ceased ;
Gone the train of knights and ladies from the dance
    and from the feast.

But the fairest and the noblest of them all has bent
    her pride,
In her chamber to keep vigil, with Almansor by her
    side

Paled and flashed her cross of opal, as Almansor
    kneeling swore ;
By a Christian oath upon it, his true love for ever-
    more.

Perfume, from a golden flasket, on Almansor's low-
    ering brow,
As in evil dreams he starteth, pours the gentle
    ladye now,

For he dreams they stand together 'neath the clus-
    tered columns fair—
Of the cloister at Cordova, 'at the vesper hour of
    prayer.

Tenderly her gentle kisses, on his dark brow bent
   in pain,
Doth she press, that gentle lady—but the ill fit
   works again.

In his dream the giant pillars of the cloister shadows
   grim,
Seem to murmer hoarse displeasure at his Christian
   bride and him.

Tears that stream in bitter sorrow from her bright
   eyes, falling fast,
Weeps the Ladye o'er her lover—and the dark spell
   yields at last;

Love nor kisses could control them, spells of byegone
   Pagan years.
Vain all else! but lo! the Christian hath baptised
   him with her tears!

RETURNED FROM SEA.

AWAKE, awake, my bonny Kate!
   And once again be blythe and gay,
I'm waiting by your garden gate,
   As in the years long past away.

Awake! there is so much to tell
  Since last we two have talked together—
So many a yarn of what befel,
  In far off seas and stormy weather!

Through every watch alow, aloft,
  One thought within my heart had power—
Dear love, you little dreamed how oft
  I've looked to home and this glad hour.

Then, quickly wake, my own sweet Kate,
  And, like yourself, be blythe and gay—
The roses at your garden-gate
  Make years past seem like yesterday.

You keep me waiting as of old,
  And linger many a minute through—
And when I least expect, behold!
  A sudden flash of white and blue!—

A gleam of hair and heaven-like eyes—
  A face joy-flushed and wet with tears,
And mine to kiss and mine to prize,
  My own long-looked for through the years.

Then come, come, come, my true love Kate,
  Be mine this merry summer day—
The good God gives at last, though late,
  The happy hours for which we pray.

And yet—and yet—how well I know,
  That she whose name I call in vain,
Within that house a year ago,
  Has sung her last light-hearted strain.

So weave I dreams of lost delight,
  And for her presence idly yearn—
Who passed that gate—once, robed in white,
  Through which she will no more return!

January 26, 1880.

LEILA.

QUEEN-LIKE pride and saint-like sweetness—
  Grace as of the cypress tree—
Let my verse enshrine the picture,
  Leila, for the years to be !

Pride that bends to greet my coming,
  With a stoop-to-conquer spell ;
The tiara of her tresses,
  Which the gold clasps grace so well.

Sweetness of a soul untroubled,
  Who can tell what thoughts arise—
Heaven or dinner, Love or bonnets—
  In the blue depths of her eyes.

Grace that drapes with more than beauty
   The hid form that seems so fair—
Gems to match the roseate colour,
   Gold to bind the dark-brown hair.

Too fair picture " of the period ! "
   What a charm would it impart
To a nature nearly perfect,
   Had she only any heart.

GRACIE.—(1870–1875).

No. 1.—L'Amour qui Passe.

Stray waifs of perfume yesterday
   With art-made scent recalled the prime
Of spring, and Her, long years away,
   Who loved me well, when she had time,
And I looked back through Life's career,
   Sad-thoughted, to that long ago—
The worn-out almanac of the year
   When we two loved each other so.

Once more, as in the years gone by,
   I see your little garret-room
So near to heaven—I mean the sky !
   So sweet—with poison or perfume ?

Once more the ballet hour prolong,
  Half drowned, like Clarence, in champagne,
In which your voice, through many a song,
  To dip her drooping wings was fain !

Fair feet that trod the cul-de-sac,
  Where have ye wandered, in what ways ?
Bright eyes, through tears have ye looked back
  Upon those careless, reckless days ?
And you or I, what tempts us still ?
  Are we of those wild ways yet fain ?
The love that went with the wind's will, ·
  The youth that comes not back again.

Light loves of wasted youth, adieu !
  Vain blossom of the days that were—
In Life's closed page, best hid from view !
  And yet the poor dead flower was fair ;
No summer shall with bloom endow
  Those pressed and faded petals more,
And only dreams can sometimes now
  That " Paradise Lost" of youth restore.

No. 2.—APRÈS (1875).

SHE is dead, that we laughed with so often,
  And all that we thought was so fair,
Is a thing shut away in a coffin,
  Leaving only this lock of gold hair.

She is gone, "requiescat in pace,"
   A point on which least said is best!—
Yet at last, little golden-haired Gracie,
   May your feet that have strayed, be at rest!

Can we grieve for her, think with regretting
   Of that life not of heart or of brain—
With its innocent trick of coquetting,
   And its trifling tendresse for champagne!

Mere beauty, mere youth, we have buried,
   No heart but a pulse has been stilled—
By no love-chace those fair feet were hurried
   On the passionate pace that has killed !

She leaves, to buy back our affection,
   Only the gold of her hair !
Dead flower !   But what Spring's resurrection
   Shall shew us another as fair !

ANNIE.

" Varium et mutabile semper." —VIRGIL.

FAIREST one, in form and feature—
Captious, cruel, cross-grained creature !

In whose bright eyes' gentle greeting—
All kind thoughts rise at our meeting.

In whose face the quick flush starting,
Soon foretells our angry parting—

Sweet one, true to Virgil's " semper,"
Looks her best when in a temper ;

Rich red lips ! since first I knew them,
What unkind words have passed through them !

Little hand, no harder hitter,
Writing words than blows more bitter ;

Little feet, whose boots ambitious
Love to light on paths suspicious—

Paths that far on Life's wild highway
Lead where her way parts from my way.

Void of heart, soul, conscience, duty !—
What is good in you but Beauty ?

WRITTEN IN AN ALBUM.

For one whose face, whose form, whose voice make
    better Life's brief space,
Of all wild things one says or sings, now which one
    shall I trace ?
To bid all sorrow fly her path, all-bright be all her
    hours,

Her life, a witch's garden in midwinter filled with
    flowers ?
Ah, no, not so, one strain of pain that gentle life
    must know,
It is the cry of joy above, the sob of pain below ;
Sweet lips, pure loving heart, Love's cup but holds
    Love's poisoned wine,
And yet who fails or fears to drink, knows not the
    Powers Divine.

TO H. M. L. M.

TAKE this book of verses, born,
Like yourself, on a May morn ;
Like yourself and sister May,
Sometimes with too much to say—
Uncontrolled and spoiled unduly,
Yet who speaks her true thought truly,
With free heart that does not fail,
Though the Philistines prevail.
Take this book ;—within it gleams
Mirth much sadder than it seems ;
Song from classic story caught,
Light lay marking serious thought.
Take the verses ; both in you and them
Much, alas ! resembles C. P. M.

ENGLISH AND LATIN

WHAT is life ?
  What good gift giving ?
Storm and strife,
  Scarce worth the living
Birth, death, bridal—
  All is idle !

Love—the Sphinx
  Whom each romancer
Fondly thinks
  That he can answer—
The riddle in whose ruthless eyes
  Who fails to answer—dies.

No. 2.—LATIN.

QUID est vita ?
  Quid nos sumus ?
Via trita—
  Labor—fumus !
Heu sensistis
  Quam sit tristis.

Quid est Amor ?
  Sphinx in myrto—

Vocis clamor
In deserto.
Gratum fatum! donum datum!
Vanitasque vanitatum!

No. 3.

Miror sitne dies an Vesperis umbra, cubili
  Grata per antra, tuo, Lux mea, perque domos?
Sive dies an Vesper adest, venit omnis amori
  Tempestiva dies, Vespera grata venit.
Si concessa mihi tam dulcis rideat hora
  Tum loca loeta prius tam bene nota, petam,
Nec, si fata vetant concedere munus amanti,
  Elysium linquens, immemor exul ero.

Toronto, ante diem iv. Kal. Mai, MDCCCLXXX.

LAURA.—(1861–1865).

No. 1.—PUTTING OUT TO SEA.

Wierd night, that fallest on fading hill and meadow,
That dark and threatening o'er our course art thrown!
Does one I love look sad beneath thy shadow,
      Now I am gone?

Wild, restless wind, that through our shrouds art
    driven,
Say has she listened to thy stormy tone ?
Will she be lonely through the long, dark even,
          Now I am gone ?

Bright star that cloud can dim or tempest never,
What is thy promise in yon heaven to me ?
She loves thee, true forever and forever !
          God grant it be.

No. 2.—Eveleen.

My own girl at home,
    Weep no longer for me ;
The ship steps through the ocean foam,
    That bears me back to thee.
Full sail and bending mast,
    We cleave the waters green,
In hasting home to you at last,
    My own Eveleen.

Of you how many a night
    I've dreamed the dark watch through,
From noon's brain-searing shafts of light
    My thoughts have flown to you :
To you, in your own home bowers,
    Where the light falls cool and green ;

My saint of saints—my flower of flowers,
  My own Eveleen.

I have o'erpast the fate
  That severed us so long ;
I have o'ercome the treacherous hate,
  Forgot the rankling wrong.
I am speeding o'er the sea
  They swore should roll between
The one who loves thee well, and thee,
  My own Eveleen.

But now no longer pine—
  No longer wait and weep ;
Our pennant floats far o'er the brine,
  We march along the deep ;
With gems and royal gold,
  With silks of sunny sheen,
And bridal raimnent fit to fold
  My own Eveleen.

An hour—and he shall trace
  The old home scene once more,
But to have seen his true-love's face,
  White as the shroud she wore.
Oh, fading human love,
  Which is not, but has been !
Oh, colder than the stone above
  Thy grave, Eveleen !

No. 3.—Memory of a Loss.

Do ye ask back the shade your leaves have given,
  O trees, from yon bleak sky ?
Dost wail, wild wind, that weed and flower are driven
  Alike unheeded by ?

Wail on ! To me there came, with fate's fell power,
  A darker, wintrier day—
A sweeter summer breath, a fairer flower,
  A dawn of dearer hope, it bore away.

No. 4.—From Far.

I DREAMED that youth returned,—the unreturning !
  I saw her cottage on the high hill stand ;
And by broad waters in the sunset burning,
  I walked once more with Laura, hand in hand.

How firmly fashioned is the tiny figure,
  Her keen grey eyes, how fairy-like they glow ;
She stands, her light limbs full of grace and vigour,
  Her hand close claspt in mine, as long ago !

It is not love upon my senses stealing,
  My thoughts no purpose and no pause allow ;
No passion blends with the intenser feeling,
  As once again I kiss that fair young brow.

D

Enchantment streamed once more on hill and ether,
    Beneath us ocean seemed a summer sea;
" Be mine," I said, and let us go together,
    That I once more may pure and happy be.

But what her words were I cannot remember,
    For suddenly awaking, I lay here,
In this bleak land whose May might match December,
    The sullen spring-time of a flowerless year.

No. 5.—SOUTH AFRICA REMEMBERED AT NIAGARA,
CANADA.

WIND of the South, hast thou stolen the breath of
    the blossoming heather,
    Fresh from the land I left, never again to return !
Bringing me back the days, when, walking over the
    hill-side,
    Many a time we met, we who shall meet not again !
There are the myrtles still, there twine the clamber-
    ing roses
    Garden and granite cliff, there are they still as of
    old !
There by the wine-dark sea, dark bloom Constantia's
    vineyards,
    There are the tall black ships, moored in the mir-
    roring wave,

Changeless all and fair, as then when last I beheld
   them
  Faintly with farewell gaze, over the heave of the
   sea—
Changeless, though but a dream ; still fair, though
   but an illusion,
  Seen through the torrent's sweep, heard through
   the cataract's roar.

VERSES WRITTEN IN COLLEGE DAYS.

KILLINEY STRAND.

(Written at sea in the tropics, 1864.)

WELL ! that heat, thirst, and headache could torture
   one so,
  I dreamed not in former years ;
When one's pulse is a glow, when one's brain and
   one's brow
  The fire of the fever sears ;
When again and again, though the thought brings
   pain,
  I long for the lost home-land,
And the joys long fled with the days that are dead,
  By fair Killiney's strand ;

With the sunny days now dark and dead,
  By fair Killiney's strand.

O glorious and golden time,
  For love and for song and carouse!
O ghost of happiness, crowned sublime
  With saddest of cypress boughs!
O period of "smiles and wine,"
  Two things it is hard to withstand,
And that turned my head in the days that are dead,
  By fair Killiney's strand;
In the sunny days now dark and dead,
  By fair Killiney's strand.

Vain complainers are those
  Who lament for the lost happy hours—
In this wine-stream of amber and rose
  Live the spring and the flowers!
Lives the love in this magical stream!
  Will it kindle again at command?
Ah, but feebly instead of the Spring that is fled
  By fair Killiney's strand!
Ah, how faintly instead of the fire that is dead
  By fair Killiney's strand.

A BOY'S IDEAL.

THOU faithful one, in cloud or calm for ever by my
  side,   .
O, constant still when all are changed, O, true what-
  e'er betide ;
Companion in the heaven of dreams, the hope of
  better years—
Consoler in this waking world of sorrow, pain and
  tears !

And yet, as I have fancied oft, that brighter time
  may be,
When happiness and human love reveal themselves
  in thee ;
Thou yearned-for form and beautiful, that livest but
  in my dreams,
And yet with hours that give thee life the mystic
  future teems.

And other's eyes look strange on mine, and other's
  words are cold,
But thine are lustrous with the love I yearned for
  oft of old ;
Thy unseen presence haunts my path. I hear not,
  neither see
A sound or shape of beauty but it tells my heart of
  thee,   .

I know not. All things are a dream that fades and
   _ melts away—
Even thou, a fancy, whose bright hues are fleeting
   day by day;   .
To the heart's pure cloister only can we fly from
   life's dull throng—
The loving and the beautiful are ours alone in song.

A COLLEGE IDYL.

So through the fields he came that happy eve in the
   summer,
The sunshine aslant through the leaves had check-
   ered the light on his pathway,
And from the shrubbery round, and the bordering
   trees of her garden,
Heard he the humming of bees, and the birds' blythe
   chirp in the hedges,
So that his heart beat quick, and he leaned on the
   gate for a moment,—
Leaned on the well-known gate they had passed so
   often together.
There by the porch she sat, and the clambering roses
   above her
Clustered their flowers around her dark-brown hair
   like a halo.

So taking heart of grace at last he entered the
    garden.
Calm and smiling she rose, and said she was happy
    to see him:
Was he not tired with his walk? had he come by
    the road or the meadow?
Her book? Oh, yes! The last new volume of
    poems,
Songs of a feverish bard who doubts both Love and
    Religion,
All most morbid and wild, and yet they somehow
    amused her!

This and more, poor fellow, full many a night he
    has told me,
In the old times as we sat by the fire in College
    together,
Each with flagon and pipe, cloud-wrapt in rich
    Latakia.

BY THE SEASIDE.

WHY sittest thou by the shore,
    Emmeline!
Why sportest thou no more,
    Emmeline

'Mid those naiads of the period just emerging from
 the brine,
Those blue eyes in the blue water, why so sadly dost
 incline—
  Looking wistful or half tristful,
   Emmeline !

  One summer morn like this,
   Emmeline !
Thy heart beat close to *his*,
   Emmeline !
And I rather think he took the liberty to twine
His arm just for one moment round that slender
 form of thine ;
  O, was it not imprudent,
  In a penniless law student,
   Emmeline ?

  He loves you, the poor wretch,
   Emmeline !
But there's many a better catch,
   Emmeline !
Cut him dead when next you meet him, burn his
 letters every line,
And deserve the eligible match your dearest friends
 assign.
  He is but a poor and true man—
  You a Lady—not a Woman,
   Emmeline !

IN THE CITY STREET.

THE lamps, so lank and ghastly,
  Are flickering in the street—
And in my face more fastly,
  Is borne the blinding sleet.

As shelterless I wander,
  Without in mist and storm,
The happy fire-side yonder
  Is blazing bright and warm.

And through the fog more faintly
  The casement gleams above,
With light more pure and saintly,
  Where rests the one I love.

The homeless in the city,
  Flit by me as I pass—
A changing crowd of faces
  Beneath the shuddering gas.

The children of the city—
  The loveless, greedy mart,
That has no mother's pity
  Within her stoney heart.

And still the sight it gives me,—
  O love, a fearful sign,—

That soiled and sin-worn beauty
  Has once been pure as thine!

Lost children of the city!
  For them whom thus I see,
God give me deeper pity,   .
  With purer love for thee.

A FAREWELL—1859.

RICH blue hills, whom ere to-morrow
  Yon wild waves must hide from me—
Like a dream of joy and sorrow,
  In my memory long to be—
Walls where oft mid dance and wassail
  Kindled thoughts I dare not tell—
Strand and cliff and cold-gray castle,
  Home of all I love, farewell!

In yon homestead worn and olden,
  Thy fair form I first have seen;
O'er yon hill-side, green and golden,
  Oft our path for hours has been.
By the woods and on the heather
  Streams the sunset's parting spell—
Where we last have walked together,
  Yet to thee, and all—farewell,

Rent before the fierce wind's anger,
   Our good ship's brave masts may be;
Suns may burn and foes endanger,
   Mid that far off eastern sea;
But when all is past and over,
   Safe at home, if once we lie—
Then, if years have won thy lover
   To aught dearer, let me die.

IN THE NIGHT.

In the night when the desolate sea waves are foam-
   ing,
A youth in despair and unrest has been roaming;
   In his heart—in his brain,
   There is doubt—there is pain,
And he cries to the waves in wild questioning strain.

   Oh, give me assistance
To solve this strange torturing problem, Existence!
   Oh, solve to me lucidly
This riddle called Man, that has bothered all ages so
   deucedly;
This problem which puzzles all thinkers, teachers
   and writers,

And has made their heads ache under hats, caps,
    and turbans and mitres!
    WHENCE cometh he, WHITHER shall wander?
And who dwells in the gold-gleaming star-shine up
    yonder?

    In vain!
The waves murmur in their monotonous strain,
    Fond fool and romancer,
Does he wait on the shore for an answer?

LONG DESERTED.

    YON old house in moonlight sleeping,
      Once it held a lady fair,
    Long ago she left it weeping,
      Still the old house standeth there—
That old pauper house unmeet for the pleasant
    village street! •

    With its eyeless window-sockets,
      And its courts all grass-o'er-grown—
    And the weeds above its doorway,
      Where the flowers are carved in stone—
And its chimneys lank and high, so like tombs
    upon the sky.

Ruined past all care and trouble,
   Like the heir of some old race,
When past glories but redouble
   Present downfall and disgrace—
For whom none are left that bear hope or sorrow
   anywhere.

Lost old home! and I was happy
   'Neath thy shade and summer night,
When, on one that walked beside me,
   Gazed I by the lingering light
In the depths of her dark eyes, searching for my
   destinies.

There, within our quiet garden
   Fell that last of summer eves,
Mid the gold of the laburnum,
   And the thickening lilac leaves—
Then the winter winds are now sighing round
   each leafless bough.

Haunted House? and do they whisper,
   That the winter moon-rays show—
Glancing through thy halls—a ghastly
   Phantasy of long ago?
And thy windows glancing bright with a spectral
   gala light.

Vain and idle superstition !
Thee no spectral rays illume—
But one shape of gentlest beauty,
Paceth there amid the gloom,
In whose sad eyes I can see ghosts that haunt my
memory.

AWAY!

AWAY ! for strange voices of music,
Call me afar, and I stand
Where, by the mystical Ganges,
Lieth a beautiful land.

There are the forests for ever,
Still as some strange god's shrine—
There in the calm of the river
Naiad-like lilies recline.

There in the sacred silence,
I would rest by the Ganges' stream;
Under the palm trees' shadow,
Dreaming a happy dream.

NOW.

Now thy lips are glowing red,
They will soon be cold and dead;
Strong is passion's pulse to-day,
Soon shall it be stilled for aye.

All our world of youth and love,
Weeds must soon grow rank above,
And the form we clasp be known
Henceforth in our dreams alone.

1858.

CHANGE.

Where are ye fled away,
    Bright hours of old ?
Why is the summer day
    Clouded and cold.

Why stricken thus and bent
    Do violets close ?—
Why doth a corpse-like scent
    Dwell on the rose.

Why changed and joyless now
    Must all things be ?
Because Love, for ever thou,
    Art changed to me !

                                    1858.

SOME ONE COMES.

SOME one comes, I hear the footsteps,
    See the shadow cast,
At my lonely door that trembles
    In the bitter blast—
Some one comes—or is it fancy,
    Or a friend at last.

" Open quick, so fast the snow-flakes
    Fleck the winter sky !
Let me in ! the storm increases
    As the night draws nigh—
Shelter ! quick ! no corpse is colder
    In the grave than I."

" I am Wealth, and I can give thee
    Gold that men adore—
Friends and troops of merry comrades,
    Joyous as of yore."

Fool ! will all thou hast to offer,
  Vanished youth restore ?

" I am Love, whom years that vanish,
  Still shall find the same !"
Still ! as when in Southern sunshine
First the phantom came ?
With a fond word, long unspoken—
A forgotten name !

" I am Death, I only offer
  Peace—the long day done,
Follow me into the darkness"—
Welcome ! Friend, lead on—
Only spare my dog ; let something
Grieve, when I am gone !

WERE I A KING.

(Altered from Victor Hugo.)

WERE I a king, I'd give my royal pride—
My guards steel-clad, my statesmen tried and true,
My golden throne, my porphyry chamber wide—
My realm from silver sea to mountains blue,
  For one kind look from you.

E

Were I a God, I'd give my angel choirs—
My heavens that tremble with the starry dew,
My demons chained beneath the penal fires,
And time and space, the old world and the new,
To be once kissed by you.

I DREAMED.

(Altered from Heine.)

I DREAMED as I lay sleeping,
That the old time brought back you and me !
I woke, and I was weeping,
Aye ! weeping bitterly.

And once again in my dreaming,
I thought you were laid in your grave ;
I woke, and my sad tears were streaming,
So deep was the anguish it gave.

And once, once again in my slumber,
I dreamed you were mine at the last ;
I woke, and the tears, without number,
Were falling warm and fast.

THE RIVER.

At home once more, and the sunset
  With its old familiar gleam,
Fell far on the distant city,
  And near on the quiet stream—
On the city far off, of the living,
  So fair in the distance seen;
On the city beside me, silent,
  Where the graves lie calm and green.
It glanced like gold on the woodlands,
  With silver it touched the waves,
And lit with a heavenly halo,
  That garden of quiet graves.

But within my heart was no sunshine,
  In answering brightness there,
But a heavy, questioning spirit,
  World-worn and oppressed with care;
For the scenes that were most familiar,
  Were saddest of all to see,
And a change had come over all things
  That e'er had been dear to me.
There had passed from my life a brightness,
  A joy from the days before,
And I said " to the great world-city
  I will go on my way once more—

But first, for an hour of the twilight,
　I will walk in the churchyard fair,
Peradventure to keep as a relic
　The thoughts that shall meet me there."

By the churchyard slope the River,
　Red with the sunset-wine,
By sombre cypress and willow,
　Wavered a golden line—
And I thought as I heard its murmur,
　How oft in the years long fled,
Its quiet voice had been blended
　With the service for the dead.
Full of mysterious secrets,
　Yet tender it seemed and dear,
Like the voice of an unseen Presence,
　Whose message I needs must hear.

The River! I hear it telling
　Of a young life's blighted joy,
Where the white cross guards his cradle,—
　Our little gold-haired boy;
Of the morn when he passed and faded,
　In a smiling slumber deep,
His soft blue eyes scarce curtained
　By film of the last long sleep;
For the hand of a guardian angel,
　Ere touch of the earth could stain

The blossom, to Eden bore it,
  Wet with baptismal rain.
But I thought of my own lost childhood,
  So far and so long ago,
And I said in my heart, "O River!
  Thank God! it is better so."

Again the River! it lures me,
  To look on you cross-crowned stone,
When I read how the dark cloud shadowed
  A summer of girlhood flown;
That summer of flower and promise,
  For evermore past away,
With the merry voice and the music
  Of life's bright bye-gone day.
She lies with her blue eyes' beauty
  Scarce hid by the lashes long,
She lies with her pale lips parted,
  As ready to break in song;
And still while her sleep is guarded
  By the cross she loved so well,
Each flower of the church's garland,
  Like beads, the seasons tell;   •
Then linger the violets latest,
  And there from the surpliced snow,
Wakes first with the spring's resurrection
  The crocus' golden glow.

And there at the joyous Easter,
  Stand lilies in white array,
And the " Star of St. Joseph " beameth,
  " St. Alice's bells" are gay.
And I said, " it is well, God rest her,"
  And I looked with a fervent prayer
Into heaven so blue and distant,
  And thought " may we yet meet *there!*"

IN MEMORY OF MARY D——,

WHO DIED SUDDENLY AT TORONTO IN THE SUMMER OF 1873.

This young lady was much beloved, and had helped the author at a
Sunday School feast two days before her sudden death.

O, BRIGHT young life—the fairest
  In all our festal day ;
The gayest 'mid that music
  Of boys and girls at play.
To whom none thought how sudden
  The summons Home should be !
While yet the heart was stainless,
  The fair brow sorrow-free,

But now in joyous worship,
　Where late with votive flowers
We decked the festal altar,
　Her voice was blent with ours.
But now amid our pastime
　Her merry voice rang free,
Our guest whose beauty brightened
　The children's hour of glee.

Yet darkness comes and silence!
　And years to dust that bring
The pomp of earthly worship,
　To dust the lips that sing!
And sin and care shall shadow
　The brows so bright to-day,
And for the song be silence,
　And for the flowers, decay!

"No! through the years eternal
　They shall not cease that sing
The pauseless Alleluia!
　The crowned, before the King!
And never wanes the brightness
　Of Paradisal morn,
Where bloom the virgin lilies,
　Before the Virgin-born!"

But here the ranks are broken,
　The bright hour is gone by,

And Home to Home re-echoes
   The vain and bitter cry;
That better life above us
   Makes worse the life below,
And that bright Heaven you promise
   Is to poor earth a foe.
January 27, 1880.

M. S.

Rudolph Thomas Seigfried, Professor of Sanscrit in Trinity College,
Dublin, 1856–1862.

NOT unremembered be the hours when first—
   Students of lore unvalued by the throng—
   We traced the tale of Damayanti's wrong,—
A scanty band of scholars long dispersed;
Or when the library's dim aisles we two
   Have searched together half a summer's day,
Or walking homeward the fair city through,
   By the Cathedral precinct, sombre grey,
We watched the Dublin hills in distance blue.
   O, friend, so soon, so early called away,
From all that Fortune promised, Genius gave!
   In memory of old times, this verse shall claim
   To breathe once more a not unhonoured name,
To wipe the dust from no forgotten grave.
TORONTO, April, 1880.

TO MY WIFE.

THROUGH many a chance, in many lands, we two
Have watched the side-scenes of life's changing day
Since your fresh youth and my first manhood knew
Our homeland's mother-city far away.
Such sorrows we have known as come to few—
My fault, not yours,—'mid all misfortunes true,
And ready still some cheering word to say,
To show some light that may our hopes renew.
All is not lost, if health be ours to aid
Escape from this dull place of durance drear,
This barren sand-strewn reach of bleak sea-mere—
Of plotting thieves and bitter tongues impure;
So may the Future see our home secure,
And on firm Temperance Hope's foundation laid.

N. B., February 28, 1880.

"TROY WAS."

TROY was.   For lo! to other music now
   Than in old days bade tower and temple rise,
   A Troy new-built of fire to all the skies,
With flaming walls o'ertoppeth Ida's brow.

Troy was! Therein shall we no more behold
  The wealth of youth that once made life so fair,
  See heaven-born love our mortal vestures wear ;
Or match with Helen's hair earth's paler gold ;
  Yet have we lived and battled not in vain.
When of that vanished day the tale is told,
If once within the hero-ranks enrolled,
  We lived their higher life of heart and brain :
  Though of a phantom beauty we were fain,
Though for a failing cause our hearts grew bold.

  January 27, 1880.

———

AFTER THE FRAGMENT OF SAPPHO.

BLESSED as the gods are blessed in heaven's com-
    pleteness,
  Who, sitting silent in his place so near you,
Can, as I can not, soul of perfect sweetness !
    See you and hear you.

Like the lone apple to the tree-top clinging,
  Sought by some, plucked by none, in all the
    garden,
Soon Love, who keeps thee for his day, joy-bringing,
    Shall be thy warden.

SONNET.

O WEARY current of life's languid tide !
 O phantom days that pass and perish so !
 Idols of camp, cave, mart, that come and go,
One form, now seen no more, shall still abide.
And me, though dust and final darkness hide,
 Thus much of mine survive me, that whoso
 Would see her then, to him this verse shall show
White wealth of breast and form of queen-like pride.
So when this poor life-drama's tale is told,
 And with the scene the actor disappears,
Be love unfettered, though by Death set free—
 To kiss the flower of her mouth's perfect mould,
To gaze without rebuke, where, through the years,
 Those pure, blue eyes the better life foresee.

TWO STANZAS OF MODERN THOUGHT.

PESSIMISM.

O WEARY heart, O restless heart,
 O void of strength and will—
O wild and wayward as thou art,
 I would that thou wert still.

If *here* there be no Love to sooth—
If *there* no Power to save,
I would that thou wert quiet now,
Within the quiet grave.

OPTIMISM.

CONTENT thee! be the evil hour
    Sufficient for its day,
And take in peace from passion's power,
    Thy solitary way.
Good Lady Fate, or soon or late,
    Will help us with the knife—
For Doctor Death to amputate
    The cancer we call life.

ON THE ABOVE.

WILD words of wayward song and half unmeant!
    For sure the weary Optimist's laugh but keeps
    Fit measure to the Pessimist that weeps
His *tour de force* of ceaseless discontent.
    The law of rythm through all existence sent—
    The pause of life's great heart that beateth stil
Appoints to us like change of good and ill.
    " Good " could not be without its complement,

For light's relief we need the darkness still :
Not good nor bad is life, but both are blent
In equipoise. How—He alone can tell
To whom this day these grateful thoughts up-sent.
Give thanks that wife and little children dwell
At last safe-harboured from the fever-spell.

Toronto, March 27, 1880.

A LOST TALE OF MILETUS.

Cleon, the namesake of the greater Cleon—
Though politics he shunned, in this was like him,
He dealt in leather, boots was skilled to make,
    Or when entreated, mend.

To whom one day, over a bowl of Chian,
Much grieved, complained his loving wife Mylissa,
" Peplus or Chiton, I, from time æonian,
    Have nothing new to wear.

In purple see the tailor's wife Euterpe,
In gold and amber struts the tanner's Lyce,
For me, in rags, may Aphrodite punish
    Thee, basest of mankind ! "

Next day, to all his craft gave Cleon notice,
" Thus with good Fortune.   For one Talent's fee,
I teach to all who pay me for the secret,
    How, in a single day,

To make a hundred pairs of shoes complete."
In crowds the craftsmen from the leather street,
Tanners and cobblers, sturdy sandal-menders,
    To Cleon's house they came.

Thus to them, having paid their fees, said Cleon,
" To make a hundred pair of shoes instanter—
Ye need but take a hundred pair of boots,
    And cut off all the tops ! "

Home growling went the baffled leather-sellers,
And from a Syrian mart did Cleon purchase
A purple peplus, wrought with gold and amber,
    For his Mylissa's wear.

MURRAY, Ont., 1879.

THE TWO PARSONS.

AN old song, somewhat altered, to suit events of late,
Of a fine old do-nothing Parson, who lived at a boun-
    tiful rate,
And was a staunch old Tory, and swore by Church
    and State,

And drank the glorious memory of sixteen eighty-
    eight—
        Like a Parson of the old school,
        And a old school Parson.

With a fine old peal of bells, except on Sunday, never
    hung for prayer,
With a fine old scarlet hunting coat, which he greatly
    loved to wear,
With a fine old church which needed restoration
    and repair,
And a fine old chancel, almost by the wind and rain
    laid bare—
        Like a Parson of the old school,
        And an old school Parson.

Who, drinking too much fine old port one day with
    Squire Jones,
Died of apoplexy, as all the parish owns,
And his successor announced his coming, in a letter
    dated, "*nones,*
On ye Feast of ye translation of Saint Symphorosa's
bones"—
        Like a Parson of the new school,
        And a new school Parson.

Who, to reconstruct the parish, took a new and dif-
    ferent way,
And insisted upon double choral service every day,

And with candles, copes and crosses, made a won-
   derful display,
And went on in a manner that made most people
   curse instead of pray—
      Like a Parson of the new school,
      And a new school Parson.

Till to the Court of Arches they brought this erring
   ecclesiastic,
Because they thought his prayers too long, and his
   piety too gymnastic
When Sir H. J. Fust, as every one must, condemned
   his *poses* plastic,
And his reading of the "Articles," as entirely too
   elastic—
      Like a Parson of the new school,
      And a new school Parson.

Who, to give up his living was ordered very soon,
And then against his Archbishop swore, like a
   Dutchman or dragoon,
And who went to Rome on a pilgrimage, with staff
   and sandal shoon—
And at parting was greeted with words that refer to
   a Connaughtman and to a spoon—
      Like a Parson of the new school,
      And a new school Parson.

13, TRINITY COLLEGE, Dublin, 1859.

PREFACE TO "ARTHUR CECIL PAYNE,"

Being a note on the modern art of Poetry.

The following imitations are written in no spirit of irreverence for the great poet, whose style is in some unimportant
peculiarities, parodied, otherwise the Senior Partner in the pro-
duction of this joint work would fail to represent the feeling
of gratitude and respect entertained by himself (the Senior
only in respect of age), as well as by the Junior Partner, towards those illustrious lyric poets who have made the last fif-
teen years a new era in English song. Surely "The Splendid
Shilling" was written in a spirit of no irreverence towards the
Miltonic epic, nor did the "Schoolmistress" and the "Castle
of Indolence" display want of appreciation towards Spenser's
Odyssey of Fairy Land. To parody the poems whose unap-
proachable beauty the parodist feels, perhaps, more keenly
than most others, is due to a tendency in our nature like that
which leads us to say hard things—words of mock deprecia-
tion—to lovers or children.

The following ballad presents a dialogue "of growing force"
between "Cousin Carrie" and "Little Bobby," resting on
the fact of an engagement formerly subsisting between Miss
Carrie and Mr. Jones, the unseen subject of the poem. The
latter is ill, certain patent pills are absolutely needed for his
restoration, and these can only be procured at the drug store of
which Carrie, to whom he has behaved very badly, is proprie-
tress. The illness is represented as caused by Carrie—like a mediæval witch—having made a wax image of her faithless lover.

"WHY did you make your man of wax,
Cousin Carrie ?
And stick him all over with carpet tacks ?"
"Because with my heart he had made tracks,
Little Bobbie."

F

" It is Smith of Smithsville drives so fast !
                    Cousin Carrie,
For I know his grey mare as she staggers past."
" He shall pay for his postage stamps at last !
                    Little Bobbie ? "

" He says that his cousin Jones is ill,
                    Little Carrie,
And wants you to send him your patent pill."
" He gave me a pill that was bitterer still,
                    Little Bobbie ! "

" It is Thomson of Thomsontown comes by the boat,
                    Cousin Carrie !
For I see his white hat and his dollar dust-coat."
" We shall see that that sort of a hair-pin won't
    float,
                    Little Bobbie ! "

" He sends a cent stamp and two bogus dimes,
                    Cousin Carrie,
And bids you remember the dance at old Grimes."
" When next we meet we'll have gay times,
        .   Little Bobbie."

" It is Jones' father, the Reverend Jones !
                    Cousin Carrie,
For I know the dread sound of his sermon tones."
" Then blame my cats if the corn he owns !
                    Little Bobbie."

"Oh, give him the pills in a pill-box fast,
Cousin Carrie,
Or he'll preach and exhort until dinner time's past."
"Then give him the pills—'tis my hour at last,
Little Bobbie."

"Oh, who is this sick man, so white in the gills?
Cousin Carrie,
Is it Love that consumes him or liquor that kills?"
"'Tis my fellow, that fraud—and he's taken the
pills!!! ·
Little Bobbie!"

Dissatisfied with this effort, a new start was made, apropos of the
Wife's Sister Bill, "For the abolition of Aunts:"

Sleep little toad, in your cot,
Or, although you're the image of Frank,
In your ivory form is a spot
Which your Aunt will most speedily spank.
As they won't let me marry your Pa,
You've just got the Senate to thank—

But this seeming somehow inadequate to express the feelings of an
Aunt yearning to become a ready-made mother, the Senior Partner
determined to adopt the obscure style of a philosophic poet, the
greatest since he of the Atheistic Atoms took that disastrous *tinct.*
canth.:

Rabbi ben Ezra said, "above Sordello's tomb
Sun-kindled, earth-be-mocked, eternal star flowers
bloom,
But who can solve the deep, dark problem we enquire
Why, when I kiss Fifine, I do not please Elvire?

This was too profound.   Another effort was made in the style of a
poetess, whose voluminous rhymes some men, and a good many women, profess to admire :

Down along the dingle, I was writing verses, oh !
Ding and ring and jingle, nothing sound or terse
    is, oh !
All about a fellow rich enough to marry me,
But o'er the flowerbeds yellow of love, he could
    not carry me.

But on discovering his want of that "sweet unreasonableness" in
verse writing, in which sense and sound are so "divided," the
Senior Partner made a supreme effort :

At the tinkle of the tea-tray, mid "high-tone" and
    dresses low,
When the cakes and buttered biscuits softly come
    and softly go,
Will you think upon your promise, sweet as pie crust,
    long ago ?
How you talked with me so nicely, in your gentle
    voice and low,

Told me tender tarradiddles, all whose thinness none
    might know,
With no better hair-pin near you, for *my* funeral you
    would go !
Best for me ? you bet, my darling ! best for you ? I
    guess that's so.
Think of me ? not much, since "thinking" is not in
    your line you know.

He next tried to attain to the metre (?) of the profound author of
" Leaves of Tobacco :"

Here am I, the man who utters songs to you, O pio-
neers, O loafers,
Loving you every one, and persuaded of a surety
that you are true men ;
Hating every mother's son of you, and convinced
that he is a humbug and a liar.
Here am I, the self-explicatory, the self-contradic-
tory, believing all things, believing nothing,
Disbelieving in the Church, in the Gospel, in Politi-
cal Economy, in common sense—
Believing in the politics of Kearney ; in the wisdom
of Elias Hicks, in the oracles rapped out by a
dollar medium.

But this metre, invented in the tenth century—the darkest of the
mediæval night—by NOTHER, has been quite sufficiently elaborated
by TUPPER and WHITMAN.. A gentler strain was suggested by the
rhythm of "The Lord of Burleigh :"

Maids who go to matins daily !
    Of a curate, hear me tell,
Mild as milk and sound as Paley,
    One, methinks, would suit you well.

She, too, daily went to matins,
    Chanting the Gregorian tones ;
And she dressed in silks and satins,
    And her name was Martha Jones.

This, however, seemed to trench on the province of the ecclesiastical novels. It being in the present mode with one of our greatest poets to include French and Latin lyrics in his work, and a sufficiency of the latter having been already given, the following was attempted :

> *Ce petit livre, O ma chere,*
> *Que Monsieur Rose a publié—*
> *C'est le tombeau, c'est la parterre*
> *Ou ma jeunesse est enterré !*
> *Et dans sa robe de blèu-royal*
> *Ma muse fidèle à repandu*
> *Le douce parfum, l'amour loyal,*
> *Des beaux jours qu'il a continu.*

Rosettian melodies dictated a poem on the moral physiology of the Flirt of the period, which would have been exhaustive, and began thus :

Light little Lottie was Love's apt scholar,
Fond of a dance, and fond of a dollar—

But the MSS. fell under the notice of a lady of prominent authority in the Senior Partner's household, who declared in unmistakable terms her disapproval of Miss Lottie's conduct, and ordered the MSS. to be consigned to cremation in the cook-stove ! Finally he hit on the metre of the following, which is at least original :

THE TRUE AND DOLEFUL HISTORY OF THE LOVES, RELIGIONS, AND WHISKERS OF MR. ARTHUR CECIL PAYNE.

" I WAS not born to lounge about an antipogonotrophist,"
Said the beardless Mr. Arthur Cecil Payne—

" I was not born to live unshorn, an Antipogono-
trophist;
With a beard and an imperial, I on Feast day,
Fast, or Ferial,
Rather think I should look anything but plain :"
Said the beardless Arthur Cecil,
This whiskerless young Arthur Cecil Payne.

So straight he off to London went, and read the
Chaetotechnicon,
Did this beardless Mr. Arthur Cecil Payne—
And bought the " Kallo-trophic oil," as bade the
Chaetotechnicon—
Using half a bottle daily, he through all the
season gaily
Waited, getting up his whiskers into train. !

One day it came to pass he heard the Rev. Mr.
Purchas preach,
Did this low church, Mr. Arthur Cecil Payne—
Providentially it came to pass he heard this Mr.
Purchas preach
Where St Mary Magdelené, spite of Cumming and
D'Aubigné,
There in London has her chapel built again ;
Then walked in this Arthur Cecil,
Then sat down this Mr. Arthur Cecil Payne.

And there before the screen, in front of Rood and
Ante-pendium,
Knelt this low church, Mr. Arthur Cecil Payne—

Where the gold "Corona Lucis" lay before the
    Ante-pendium—
Saw the *Eleemosynarium* that hung up in the
    SACRARIUM!!!
Underneath the eastern window's tinted pane—
    Then knelt down this Arthur Cecil,
This converted Mr. Arthur Cecil Payne.

And he said, " O, the young lady that can work me
    such an altar-cloth,
    Work for me, young Mr. Arthur Cecil Payne—
Such a mass of hearts and lilies, stars and crosses,
    for an altar cloth,
    Then, whatever lady knows to work me this, will
    I propose to,
For all others their flirtations shall be vain
    With me, Mr. Arthur Cecil,
    Rich and eligible Arthur Cecil Payne.

" Goodness, gracious ! " the young ladies said who
    read the letters mailed to them,
All on vellum, signed by Arthur Cecil Payne—
When they read the mediæval gothic letters that he
    mailed to them—
    " Goodness gracious, well, I never, or if so why,
    hardly ever—
Why the young man must be really insane ;
    Mad is Mr. Arthur Cecil—
Grown religious—Mr. Arthur Cecil Payne."

So the story reached at last the ears of Sister Agatha,
And she heard of Mr. Arthur Cecil Payne;
And she worked for him an altar-cloth, herself did
    Sister Agatha—
    All on silk from Hardman ordered, and with silver
        crosses bordered,
And she sent it up to Dublin by the train,
    Mailed to Mr. Arthur Cecil—
Per express to Mr. Arthur Cecil Payne.

Soon as ever he beheld it why he drove away to visit
    her,
    Wild with love, did Mr. Arthur Cecil Payne—
In a gorgeous coat from Buckmaster's, he walked up
    stairs to visit her,
    And kneeling there before her, was beginning to
        implore her,
That for ever she would condescend to reign
    In the heart of Arthur Cecil,
In the constant heart of Arthur Cecil Payne.

" By our Lady, bold young man !" she said, " I never
    heard such sacrilege,
    Bold and carnal Mr. Arthur Cecil Payne;
If others of Miss Sellon's nuns will listen to such
    sacrilege,
    Her you then perchance may marry—but for me
        I may not tarry—
For I'm hasting to my convent back again—

Far away from Arthur Cecil,
Anti-celibate young Arthur Cecil Payne."

So changed at last by grief to stone, upon the church
    at Sandymount,
Stands the altered Mr. Arthur Cecil Payne—
Miraculously there transmogrified at Sandymount,
    Unto all the Irish nation, of the evils of flirtation,
    A sad monument shall evermore remain—
    In this altered Arthur Cecil,
In this petrified young Arthur Cecil Payne.

NOTE.—These *vers de société* were written years ago in College, as
may be seen from the use of several names of those who "*abierunt
ad plures*" since then. The verses, such as they were, were written
it is hoped in a spirit of good humoured fun, and are meant to sneer
at no form of religious thought, although they may point a laugh at
the eccentricities of Party.

HYMNS ON SACRED SUBJECTS.

The following versions of favourite Hymns are the result of some years' study of the Hymns of the mediæval Church. The English originals are from Hymns A. and M. The version of "Hark! the Herald Angels Sing," was published in the First Series of Kottabos, the serial representing the University of Dublin.

WESLEY'S CHRISTMAS HYMN.

"Hark! the Herald Angels Sing."

ECCE! chorus angelorum
Surgit circa regis torum !
Pietas et Pax beata,
Lux e tenebris est data,
Surgat vox mortalium
Cum choro cœlicolum—
Dicant omnes hodie
Christum natum Virgine.

Christus, venerandum Numen !
Ex æternâ luce lumen !
Thronum deserens regalem
Alvum intrat Virginalem !

En ! per carnem Caritas !
Impermixta Deitas—
Inter homines Creator
Natus est et Mediator.

Ave ! Pacis Rex qui venis !
Sol exoriens terrenis.
Tu dedisti lumen clarum
Regioni tenebrarum.
Tu splendorum exuisti,
Causam nostram suscepisti—
Tam Creator, quam Creatus,
Et ut renascamur, Natus !

WESLEY AND MADAN'S ADVENT HYMN.

"Lo ! He comes with clouds descending."

This magnificent Hymn seems worthy to rank with the "Dies Iræ," and with the equally grand but less known—

"Apparebit repentina Magna Dies Domini ! "

The following version, written at Murray, Canada, was honoured with a place in one of the leading Church papers in England, Jan.; 1879.

En ! per nubes Rex descendit !
Qui suorum Victima,
Quondam in cruce pependit—
Et sanctorum agmina,
Mille, mille ! ducit Ille
Triumphans per æthera.

Quam in throno Majestatis
　　Omnis cernet oculus,
Quique prædam sceleratis
　　Prodiderunt hostibus—
Tum videbit et stupebit
　　Infidelis populus.

Næ! Amen! Enthronizato
　　Honor, Laus et Gloria!
Metu mortis superato
　　Regnum sit per sæcula!
Veni Christe! fini triste
　　Tempus! Alleluia!

　　　　　　　　　Amen.

Oft in danger oft in woe—
Onward, Christians, onward go!

PER pericla tristis sortis,
Perge semper, perge fortis—
Nec segnis, nec superatus
Carne Christi recreatus.

Pelle lacrymas et metus!
Illuc finietur fletus—
Quanto victus es labore
Tanto salvus sis victore.

Cor languescens adjuvetur—
Armis cæli munietur.

Pugna fortiter, nec mora—
Cantum ciet victrix hora.

Perge medias per cædes
Debellator mox incedes—
In hostilis vim cohortis,
Miles Christi, perge fortis !

Ergo laus et cantus datur
Tibi, sempeterne Pater.
Et cum sancto Jesu, quoque
Procedenti ab utroque.

"Sun of my Soul, Thou Saviour dear."

The Latin versions of this and of the preceding Hymns, were published in the *Dominion Churchman*, of Toronto, a paper to which I
am indebted also for the insertion of a series of articles on the history
of Christian Hymns.—(*Dominion Churchman*, 1878.)

SOL et Salvator animæ,
Non nox erit præsente Te !
Nec condet vis caliginis
Te a tuorum oculis.

Et me dum mulcent somnia
Tuo dono dulcissima,
Sim memor quanta qualia
Tecum Tuorum gaudia !

Adsis mihi, precor, die,
Vix vita valet sine Te,
Adsis sub noctem, nam Tuis
Tecum vix mors terribilis !

Si erret exul quis a Te
Contemptâ voce veniae,
Huic lux Tua nunc lucceat,
In Patris sinum redeat.

Infirmos, aegros, anima !
Pauperibus da munera,
Et oculis lugentium.
Infantis dulce somnium.

Surgentes Tu nos suscipe,
Vitaecque viam dirige,
Mox in Tuâ dulcedine,
Œternâ simus requie.

Amen.

FROM THE HYMN OF ST. HILDEBERT.

ME may Sion's sacred city,
Shelter from life's harms in pity,
Peaceful refuge, Ark divine !
Thou that on the Rock dost shine—
Home of safety and assistance,
I salute thee in the distance !

FROM TRENCH'S "SACRED LATIN POETRY.'

Mortis portis, fractis Fortis,
Fortior vim sustulit,
Et per crucem, regem trucem,
Infernorum perculit.

Now the gates of death are broken;
To the stronger yields the strong,
To the cross, victorious token,
Bow the powers that ruled so long.
Brightness of illumination
Flashed through realms of darkness free,
Since salvation to creation,
He who made it, willed should be.
The Creator for creation,
Saved from death, Himself, will die,
On whose dying we relying,
Hope the gift of life on high.
Thus is Satan's doom dethronement,
By the Victor's glad atonement,
That to Him with death is fraught,
By which life to man is brought.
See the captive conquering,
Priest at once and offering!
Girt with power and grace exceeding,
Smote the King the infernal reign,
In the first dawn, forth proceeding,
From the tomb He rose again.

A CHRISTMAS CAROL.

(Manner of the Thirteenth Century.)

SHEPHERDS abiding without in the cold,
(Wind on the wave and snow on the shore)
Why come ye hither so far from your fold ?
(Maidens and men rejoice evermore).

Kings from the East that are led by a Star—
(Wind on the wave and snow on the shore)
Red gold and incense why bring you from far ?
(Maidens and men rejoice evermore).

We sail over sea from the land of the Jews ;
(Wind on the wave and snow on the shore)
Of God and our Lady we give you good news—
(Maidens and men rejoice evermore).

Dark on the village the night had gone down ;
(Wind on the wave and snow on the shore)
Bleak the night-blast blew on Bethlehem town—
(Maidens and men rejoice evermore).

Suddenly, sweetly, the angel-host sings,
(Wind on the wave and snow on the shore)
Flashing through gloom with a gold-gleam of wings—
(Maidens and men rejoice evermore).

G

Sweet is the song that they sing to us still :
(Wind on the wave and snow on the shore)
"Peace upon earth unto men of good will"—
(Maidens and men rejoice evermore).

ST. MARGARET.*

(Martyred at Antioch, A.D. 325. Tune—" Allelluia, sing to Jesus.")

IN the days of heathen darkness, in the orient far
    away,
Died for Christ the Christian martyr, of whose acts
    we sing to-day ;
Flower of faith, whose earth-born beauty shall in
    fadeless bloom remain,
Pearl of price, whose cost the Merchant with His
    blood to pay was fain.

By the heathen's cruel hatred, by the torture and the
    sword,
Undismayed the Christian maiden, witness bore to
    Christ the Lord ;
With her pure, calm brow that flinched not, the long
    hours of torment through,
Till the men that killed the body, had no more that
    they could do.

---

* This and the two following lyrics are inserted simply on their
merits as poems, and are not intended to convey the author's belief in
any doctrine. They were written some years ago.

In that ancient, eastern city, many a year has passed
away,
Since the sweet eyes of the Martyr closed in blood
that dreadful day;
Since the latest prayer, "forgive them!" for her foes
her faint lips sighed,
And the pure, white form lay painless, in the death-
sleep like a bride.

Years have passed, but still shall Christians, by their
love for Margaret's name,
Worship Him whose gift the Martyr's crown and
conqueror's palm-branch came—
Grant us Lord, who sing Thy Martyr, us who find
Thy Saint so fair,
Here on earth the Martyr's courage, rest with her
victorious *there*.

THE REQUIEM HYMN.

Son of Mary, throned on high,
Far above yon stormy sky;
Yet whose human heart can tell,
Every grief of ours so well!
Man in mercy, God in power,
Help in this the darkest hour;
Who can save if Thou condemn,—
Grant a blessed Requiem.

For the little children laid,
Cradled in the church's shade ;
Whom their hour of sinless play
Tired so early in the day ;
Yet new-born and undefiled,
Safe with Mary's holy child,—
Jesu, born in Bethlehem,
Grant a blessed Requiem.

For the youth whose flower and pride,
The dark dust awhile must hide ;
Taken hence ere heart so true,
At the half its worth he knew.
Like a conquerer laid low,
By some chance stroke of the foe ;
Yet grief's deepening tide to stem,
Grant a blessed Requiem.

For the loved ones called away,
Late in life's fast-waning day ;
After many a peril past,
Many a wandering, home at last.
In that land where strife is o'er,
Sword and storm can part no more ;
From the dust we cry for them,
Grant a blessed Requiem.

So with not a hopeless creed,
For the silent lips we plead ;
So with faith's unfaltering zeal,
In the vacant place we kneel :

Earthly love before the shrine,
Of that awful Love Divine,
Still can touch the garment's hem,—
Grant a blessed Requiem.

Powers of darkness, shades of pain,
Soon shall pass your dreary reign ;
Soon a stronger overthrow
That last fastness of the foe.
Son of Mary, God most high !
Death and hell for us defy !
Thou canst save, tho' all condemn,—
Grant a blessed Requiem.

" MORITURUS SALUTO."

THOU who alone the veil
Can'st lift, that hides the nothing, or the All,
Whom as God's Angel men that hate thee feign,
' Yet from this life, ere joy that fills it, fail,
And " dust to dust," and final darkness fall,
Thy hated foot refrain !

For soon in Psyche's car
Love whispers his last secret and is dumb ;
Desire is dead as any gods ordain—
Nor, though her footfall to his grave draws near,

To the still heart she tramples on, shall come
  That rhythm of rapturous pain.

  The pulse that to her name,
In music of a sweet forbidden song,
Still kept true time, each heart-beat of the years,
Shall cease or be the blind Force whence it came—
Shall flow no more to do that Lethe wrong—
  Life's ceaseless stream of tears.

  Yet while dead Summer's wraithe—
The phantom of a vanished Sun from far—
Shines in brief brightness of the winter day,
Let love be ours, who have not Hope or Faith—
Love in whom burns no Passion's pulse to mar
  The peace of calm decay.

WHY ?

Vaguely remembered from a Sanscrit Poem, read, in 1858, with
Dr. Seigfried, then Professor of Sanscrit, University of Dublin.

WHY should the good cause fail, and the bad cause
  still be successful,
Failure be still the meed of the saints, the martyrs
  the heroes ;
Gold and all good things reward the sinners and
  swindlers ?

Why should the Truth be crushed, condemned and
    crucified always?
Why should the Lie prevail, supreme on earth and
    in heaven?
These are difficult questions only known unto Brama,
Who in the highest heaven sits throned to rule
    over all things;
Possibly Brama himself could not explain the
    enigma.

CHANGE.

They change, they die, we see them day by day
    Go past in wedding-robes and funeral hearses,
Uncaring what may fail or pass away,
    Until our little clique at last disperses.

Why do those Fates that rule us as they will,
    Still make the worst on each occasion winners?
Why do disease, and debt, and failure still
    Make us such very miserable sinners.

A life-time's toil may win what we desired,
    Just when enjoyment fails and Love grows hoary;
And those old dames, the Destinies, untired,
    Make of each human life the same sad story.

Alas! all generous hopes are over-topped
    By selfish facts, and I, a fond romancer,
May question on, until my mouth is stopped
    By church-yard dust—is this the only answer?

CANADA THANKSGIVING HYMN.

FOR the gifts the seasons yield,
Gold that crowns the harvest field ;
For our homes at peace and free,
Through the land from sea to sea ;
By nor slave nor tyrant trod,
Canada gives thanks to God.

Of Thine own we give Thee, Lord,
Thine the gifts our fields afford,
Wealth of wood and boundless plain,
Harvests heaped with golden grain ;
Room for all, and homes that see
Church and school and market free.

Twine the Font with lilies fair,
Censers of the summer air—
Childhood's flower beneath our skies,
From each poor home free to rise
To all hope of progress won,
Turned to knowledge like the sun !

Round the aisles the green wreaths twine,
Emblems of fresh Truth divine,
Free to grow unforced, unawed,
Through all symbols seeking God ;
Free for Faith and Love to plead,
In each name of human need.

Till the better day shall be,
Of a world from vice set free ;
Till the social life shall show
God revealed in man below ;
Till the star, in clearer skies,
Of our own Republic rise.

* * * *

HYMN FOR THE BURIAL OF A FRIEND'S CHILD.

WE lay thee, lost to Life's brief span,
 Beneath the sacred sod ;
Because thou art the child of man,
 We know thee child of God.

We doubt no word that Christ has said,
 Nor deem God's love a lie,
Though the young life He sinless made,
 He willed should sinless die.

We have no faith that endless hell
 Waits infants undefiled—
That God, of whom the Gospels tell,
 Could hate a little child.

And since to thee, unstained from birth,
 Death's second birth is given,
We hold that Heaven's best gift to Earth,
 Earth safe returns to Heaven.

TORONTO, March 7th, 1880.

LAST WORDS.

Go little book ! and meet what greeting Canada gives
    thee,
Good report or ill, purchasers many or few—
Go with thy verse-wreath, sought from woodland,
    river, and hillside,
    Record of fifteen years lived in the Maple Leaf
    land,
Quinté's calm blue bay, and Ottawa's hurrying
    waters,
    Or where the City Queen sits by Ontario's wave ;
Now 'mid the stately streets, and now 'mid wilder-
    ness sylvan,
    Home and mirror and bath, still of the Dryad
    unscared.
Yet they have soothed my days, those well-known
    classical echoes.
    Yet 'mid life's losses and cares, HOMER and
    HORACE were mine.
Yet in our own poor home were gleams of Beauty
    ideal—
    Weimar's sage and Ferney's, glories of Hellas and
    Rome..
Yet shall this page recall the friends that Canada
    gave me,
    Friends most true and tried, ever remembered and
    dear, .
Ballads of Faces Fair, that in the Past or Present

Read of erst or seen, lived in my fancies again.

Last, with the lighter strains, the heart's mirth born
of the moment,

Some more serious chords come from the parsonage
cell,

Sounding in fancy oft, when through the aisles of
the wildwood,

Solemn sequence and hymn heard I from ages afar;

Studied for many a year, that strange, quaint, barbarous Latin,

Monkish tomes, my work oft for a long summer
day :

Have they been lost, those hours ? those rhymes, for
what do they profit ?

Barbarous Latin at best, art of a barbarous age.

Yet to the student shall art be art, though the age be
a dark one—-

Struggling in turbid dawn on to the brightness of
day.

Art to the few so dear, so scorned by the Philistine
many—

Art which sufficeth itself ever for praise and reward.

Toronto, May, 1880.

SONNETS,

SONGS OF IMMORTALITY,

AND

STORY OF SYLVALLA.

BY

AMOS HENRY CHANDLER

SONNETS.

IN MEMORIAM.

HON. EDWARD BARRON CHANDLER, LIEUT.-GOVERNOR OF NEW BRUNS-
WICK, OBIIT. FEB. 6, 1880.

HARK to the strains! the deep, slow strains, so grand
  Yet solemn, of the "dead-march," while the knell
  From the Cathedral's spire sounds farewell:
His name among the honor'd roll shall stand,
Of Brunswick's statesmen: down, beside the strand,
  She gently bears him, whom she lov'd so well;
Whose memory ever in that heart shall dwell,
That mourns now for him, up and down the land.

Beneath her flag where he lay, hush'd, "in state,"
  Till midnight hundreds on those features gaze,
Of one who, faithful, served his country dear;
While at his home sad friends and kinsmen wait,
  Recounting his good deeds, in generous praise,
'Mid many untold—unrecorded *here.*

March 4th, 1880.

IRELAND'S FAMINE, 1880.

A CRY is heard across the wintry sea,
　　From Arra's hills beside the Shannon fair,
　　"Ierne" strikes the lyre in despair ;
Oh! listen to her wail of agony,
While starving children in great misery
　　Cling to her skirts, who cannot longer bear
　　Gaunt Famine's pangs: Haste Canada! and
　　　　share
With blest Columbia, kindly sympathy.

Lo! millions then shall heed the loud lament;
　　With messages, the light'ning swift employ,
　　Of love and pity—waft a generous store
Of largess, from the whole wide continent :
　　Make Erin's harp re-throb with tend'rest joy,
　　So often thrill'd by Carolan and Moore.

JUNE.

FAIR as the hue of Chrysoprase, in sheen
　　Of emerald light upon an angel's crest,
　　Her star-born eyes flash down upon the breast
Of throbbing earth their rays in chymic green;

O'er hill and vale, and far across the sea,
Her silver laughter through the welkin rings,
    Awaking all the praise and harmony
That dwell within all animated things:
    She weeps too; but 'tis only tears of joy
That fall in showers for her belovèd one,
    Blent with sweet smiles—'tis only the alloy
Of cloud and sunshine, since the world begun,
That makes the sum of love : From lips dew-wet
Exhales the perfume of all flowers, from rose to violet.

IN MEMORIAM.

"CLARA."

" So tired, and so weary : Oh ! my God'
    Come, take me home to Thine eternal rest :
Thy will be done : I humbly kiss the rod :
    This drooping head upon my Saviour's breast
    I fain would lean, and join th' ransomed blest. "
Thus speaks she, while angelic choirs applaud !
Oh, lay her body gently 'neath the sod,
    As sinks the sun beyond the golden west ;
    And, Winter! mantle with thy shroud of snow,
Her silent tomb ; and dove-white Seraph, Peace,

H

Thy pinions spread o'er her dear dust below!
While, upward, shining in a glorious glow
Of light immortal, welcoming release,
Her soul attains that perfect joy that nevermore
shall cease.

IN MEMORIAM.

A. J. H.

Come, enter: and with slow and solemn tread
  Approach his bier, and bid thy last adieu
  To one whose heart was ever kind and true
Step softly in the presence of the dead;
And, on the marble of his fair forehead,
  The chaplet wreathe of cypress branch and rue
  Forever green, in memory bright and new,—
Look on him once more and be comforted.
Farewell, alas! but may we never hear,
  Enchanted near—that silver tongue again,
His eloquence, his poetry of prose?
Yea! higher up, beyond the white dawn clear,
  When love and friendship shall immortal
   reign;
Beyond time, too, and all its stormy woes.

AURORA.

LED by the hand of Ashtoreth she trips
Her snowy feet along the twilight way
That skirts the eastern highlands of the bay ;
And oh, the fragrance of those rosy lips !
  And oh, the glory of those star-lit eyes,
Perfumes the emerald tresses of the Earth—
  Flecks her bright bosom with the fairest dyes,
While blend June-murmurs with lark-warbled mirth.
  Hark ! like a giant rousèd from his rest,
Auster is up ! and shakes the meads dew-wet ;
And rolls the wood and tarn, where swallows flet,
  Cooling their bills : Lo sunrise ! 'toward the west
Veil'd in a mist fresh-woven in the meads,
The goddess wings her sun-bright course and back
  to Heaven speeds.

IN MEMORIAM.

A. H.

WITH the first blossoms of the Autumn-tide
  She gently drooped ; but wherefore should we
    grieve ?
  The sweetest flowers soonest take their leave

Of this sad earth ; and saintliest souls abide
Not long, when Heaven opes its portals wide
 To welcome them! For her the cypress weave
 With those words gracious heard this Sabbath
 eve—
In whom strong faith, and good works were allied—
" She is not dead but sleepeth," Christ did say—
 Beside the damsel with all pitying love—
 To Jairus in his affliction sore
" She is not dead but sleepeth ! " Far away ;
 Safe neath the shelter of th' Almighty Dove—
She is not dead, *but lives* forevermore !

TO SIRIEL.

THOUGH cruel time and distance may divide
 Us, gentle lady ; or, though health may fade,
Or fate compel me for long years to wade
 Through seas of trouble, still *thou* shalt abide
 Within the cell, where symp'thy, side by side
With friendship of this heart, is safely laid—
Forgive this weakness, and do not upbraid
 One whom to thee 's mysteriously allied.

True as the needle throbs unto the pole ;
 Pure as the love within the mother's breast ;

Swift as the dove wings westward to her home,
Shall this heart vibrate to thy kindred soul—
   Shall be the memory of that vision blest,
Shall I speed to thee, in the great unknown.

THE DEATH-SONG OF OUHAHA.

(From the 5th Canto of the Story of Sylvalla.)

OH ! it was him alone !
Oh ! it was him alone
I lov'd with all my heart,
Dear to me yet thou art ;
' Twas for him I prepared,
Whose love so long I shared,
Over the bough-swift fires, fresh killèd meat ;
The noble deer its skin
Dress'd I ofttime for him,
Work'd too the mocassins that graced his feet.

I waited, while the sun
Circle'd all day on high,
Down to the western sky,
His return from the chase ;
As when with hasty pace

His firm and manly step heard I and knew :
    My heart rejoiced all o'er
    When he threw at the door
The deer haunch,—at once to prepare it I flew.

    This heart was bound in him !
    This heart was bound in him !
    He was the world to me,
    Dear still his memory ;
    But afar off he's gone,
    Left with another one,
Life is a burden now I cannot bear :
    Even my children three
    Add to my agony—
They do so, each one, his every look share.

    How can I longer live !
    How can I longer live !
    Lift I my voice on high,
    Manitou, hear my cry ;
    Spirit, take back my life,
    Far away from this strife !
My prayer to fulfil, lo ! the stream hastes along—
    See the white water foam—
        'Tis my shroud !   Hear the groan,
And roaring, deep below—my funeral song.

THE DEATH-SONG OF OULISSI.*

(From the 4th Canto of the Story of Sylvalla.)

LEAVE me not all alone!
Come! on the wings of night, from the star-fields of
    light
Come, oh come! spirit near—come, my Sylvalla dear,
    Soothe now my dying groan.

Low-stricken 'mid the slain,
No more the battle-hum—no more the battle drum
Shall strike upon my ear. Ha! I see hasting here,
    Circling across the plain,

War-birds of carnage red;
Near and more near they seem. Ha!'tis no idle dream—
As yonder orb 'neath the west sinks, so this fainting
    Soon shall my day be sped.   [breast—

When rose fair Peace's star
Like a calm summer sky, this face and beaming eye,
But as storm-clouds in ire, darkly and flashing fire
    Were they in time of war!

---

* " The death song of Oulissi."—After the " Battle of the Plains "
(described in the 4th Canto of the " Story of Sylvalla "), " Oulissi,"
at the hour of sunset, lies faint and bleeding on the field—invoking
the shades of his deceased wife and child, " Minnegoo," to sustain
and comfort him in his dying moments.

As every autumn leaf
Falls to the ground below, one by one'lay them low.
Micmacs! from far and wide gather ye every tribe,
Micmacs! avenge your Chief!!

Swift as the lightning blast
Casts down the forest trees, Great God, mine enemies!
Loud as the thunder-moans, be all their dying groans—
To the earth hurl and dash.

Fainting and dying now,
Star of my destiny! as these earth-shadows flee,
Star of my future life—as my past, come my wife
Over this giddy brow.

Flutter with gentle wing—
Drive off these battle-birds—hail! how thy words
Soothe this last agony: waft me where,--ha! I see
"Minnegoo" beckoning!

THE LAMENT OF SYLVALLA ON THE DEATH OF "MINNEGOO."

(From the 4th Canto.)

SAD and comfortless,
Utter loneliness
Fills my spirit; like an empty room

In the dark midnight,
All bereft of light
Is my soul—a sky-beclouded gloom
Where no stars illume.

Wearily each day
Drearily I stray,
Heeding not the gladdest forest stream ;
Neither song of birds
Nor the tender words
Of sympathy or friendship shed one gleam
Through the dark'ning dream.

Like a forest child
In the winter wild,
Wearied, faint and stricken with the frost,
Left without a friend
The needed help to lend—
Upon the waves of time a frail bark tost
And shattered—I feel lost.

But in mine agony
Oft she comes to me
To the wigwam, through the star-lit air,
When I hear rustlings
Of her silver wings ;
And behold her tresses shimmering there—
Her face angel-fair.

Oh God! if I weep,
Oh God! if I keep
Ever, ever, ever in my mind—
Even in mine eye,
Hear, forgive the cry,
Her my lost one gentle, good and kind,
Let me be resigned.

And oh! let me pray,
Let me silent stray,
Till I greet thee whom the angels bore—
Meet thee, Minnegoo,
In the starry blue—   .
See thee, and embrace thee as of yore—
Parted nevermore.

THE DEATH-SONG OF CHI-WEE-MOO.

(From the 2nd Canto of the Story of Sylvalla.)

EACH morn I wake,
Each morn I wake!
I hear the loon upon the lake—

"Chiweemoo," in the Micmac language, signifies "loon." The
Indians, like the Hebrews, often name their children after birds,
beasts, fishes, etc.

Heart-full of care,
Heart-full of care,
She cries, in notes of wild despair.

She, too, has lost,
She, too, has lost—
Her breast, with mine, is tempest-tost—
A loving mate,
A loving mate,
For whom, with me, she still doth wait.

Three moons ago,
Three moons ago—
What days—what nights of bitter woe !
They would not stay,
They would not stay—
From "camp" and "lake" both sped away.

While shone the moon,
While shone the moon —
Last night, again I heard the loon—
In sympathy,
In sympathy,
She poured her sorrows out to me.

The sun, so fair,
The sun, so fair
Shines on the lake ; and, everywhere,

The mated dove,
The mated dove,
Re-sings all day her tale of love

Oh, Manitou!
Oh, Manitou!
We both forgive them, though untrue—
Farewell! we cry,
Farewell! we cry—
'Tis our last death-song—we must die!

IN MEMORIAM.

E. MACINTOSH.

(An Elegy.)

THE BIRTH OF EMMA.

FALLING, falling were the dews of even,
Clouds and darkness settled in the west;
Calling, calling on her God in Heaven
Was that mother ere she went to rest.

Moaning, moaning through the Acadian wild-wood,
Were the winds, as leaves of autumn fell;
Groaning, groaning, wishing for the childhood
Of her babe, as fears and doubts befel.

Lightly, lightly, fairer clouds were driven
Past the moon, and up the star-lit sky ;
Brightly, brightly, eyes looked up to Heaven,
One brief prayer, then o'er the agony.

Singing, singing, though they might not hear it,
Were the angels on the morrow bright;
Winging, winging round the tender spirit
Of an infant, spotless, pure and white.

THE DEATH OF EMMA.

Slowly, slowly, sable shades were falling
Down the crimson portals of the west ;
Lowly, lowly orphan hearts were calling
For their mother, ere they went to rest.

Sadly, sadly, April winds were wailing,
Darkness reigned, where all before was light ;
Madly, madly stricken hearts were ailing,
Through the long, long weary hours of night.

Faintly, faintly shone the stars of Heaven
Through the gloomy, cold, and misty sky ;
Saintly, saintly, fitted with the leaven,
That last look of Immortality.

Praising, praising, though we might not hear it,
Were the angels on the morrow morn ;
Raising, raising up the blessed spirit
Of her body, wearied, faint, and worn.

THE DIALOGUE BETWEEN LYDIA AND HORACE.

Ad Lydiam.

HORATIUS.

WHILE I was pleasing yet to thee,
Nor one accepted more than me
Did e'er embrace your snowy breast—
Than Lydia's king I lived more blest.

LYDIA.

While you had not a greater love,
Nor Chloe Lydia shone above,
A Lydia of distinguished fame
More eminent shone than Ilia's name.

HORATIUS.

Now, Thracian Chloe's my desire,
The sweet-skilled mistress of the Lyre,
For whom from life I'd fearless part,
Should her, the Fates, spare but my heart.

LYDIA.

Dear Calais, son of noble sire,
Inflames me with a mutual fire,
For whom twice-suffered death were joy,
Would the Fates spare my Grecian boy.

HORATIUS.

But what if we past love invoke,
To bind us with a brazen yoke—
I Chloe shake off, and the door
Of Lydia welcome me once more.

LYDIA.

Though he is fairer than a star,
You light as cork—more passionate far
Than the Ionian sea, still I
Glad, in thy love, would live—would die !

THE DIALOGUE BETWEEN SYLVIUS AND LYRA.

SYLVIUS.

DARK eyes ; sweet breath ; and dewy lips,
Upon whose fragrant rosy tips
Fond Sylvius hangs, and nectar sips.

LYRA.

Blue eyes ; fair face ; and noble crest—
Safe pillow'd on whose sheltering breast
No harm can Lyra e'er molest.

SYLVIUS.

The heart thou stolest yesterday
Bring back, nor loiter on the way—
If asked to linger, tell him nay.

LYRA.

Yes ! if those kisses prized above
All others are returned in love—
If thou will pledge to faithful prove.

SYLVIUS.

I vow, and shall restore them : Fleet,
Trip on thy pretty nimble feet—
Come, quickly come, my sweet, my sweet !

LYRA.

Thy rose is withering in the drouth ;
And thirsts for thee, thy amorous mouth,
Warm, moist, and fragrant as the south.

SYLVIUS.

Fie ! truant girl—fond coaxing Dove,
Return unto your nest, my love.

LYRA.

Fie ! absent boy—forgive your Dove,
I come, to dwell for aye, my love.

To Sylvia.

FAIR form of grace
I love to trace,
In glances time cannot erase,
The love—replies,
From violet eyes :
On snowy feet,
So velvet neat,
Come, once more, to the "tryst," my sweet !

Come whisper, mine,
" Love, I am thine,"
While circling arms this neck entwine :
Again, that smile,
Dear, grant the while ;
That long warm kiss,
Thrill'd through with bliss,
As only lovers give I wis.

To Lyra.

ONCE journeying on my way through life,
I strayed in Love's fair bower,
And plucked the fairest rosebud there,
Just bursting into flower.

One eve, alas ! its petals fell,
The perfume rare retaining,
I

I sought the parent stem again,
   And found one more remaining,

Whose added fragrance heal'd this heart,
   Dispelling all the sorrow :
Droop not, sweet rose, bloom ever on,
   To-morrow, and to-morrow !

BABY CLARA.

PALE, wan, and faint,
   While the cold winds are sighing,
Baby is lying, Baby is dying !
    White and pure as the snow
    On her soft couch below.

See, late, so fair !
   Her dark eyes are drooping,
Dark wings are swooping—Death's Angel stooping—
    While a bright Seraph there,
    Waits her young soul to bear.

Winter-chill'd flower
   Whose perfume is fleeting ;
Like a lamb bleating, ere the fond greeting,
    Baby her Mother dear
    Meets in the starry spere.

FORGET ME NOT.

FORGET me not, belovèd,
    Far away,
In the rosy hour of morning,
    Oh, I pray ;
When, are full the maple hills
With the echo answering trills,
From a thousand mated hearts,
    At early day.

Forget me not, belovèd,
    O'er the sea,
In the silent summer noon
    Remember me ;
When the fragrant winds are laid
In the forest, vale, and glade,
And the birds have ceasèd singing,
    Think of me.

Forget me not, belovèd !
    Far away,
As the dews and shades are falling,
    For me pray ;
When the stars are in the sky,
And the night is speeding by,
I will dream of thee, my darling,
    Until day.

IMPROMPTU.

TO L.

" I LOVE you, I love you, I love you,"
You sweet little, dear little dove, you
 Must haste to your nest,
 On this bosom to rest
 Your downy soft breast,
For " I love you, I love you, I love you."

TO S.

 PASS tardy hours more fleet,
 My fondest love to greet,
 My dearest, sweetest sweet !

TO I.

THE roses bloom, the daisies smile, ·
I only can admire the while ;
But, the love I feel for *thine*, each day,
Can never, never fade away !

TO F.

LET August's zephyrs fan thy tender cheeks,
Where roses bloom beneath such dear, dark eyes ;
And when rude Winter, with his chilling blast,

Nips all the later blossoms in the vale,
May'st *thou* escape unharm'd his icy breath—
Oh, lady fair! the flower of Cumberland.

TO F.

ADIEU, my sister dear,
    Though in name only, here
Within this breast thou hast a brother's heart:
Should fate prove undeceiving, we but part
    To meet ofttime again,
    Before the evening's wane
Of this our morning: Dear, I shall remain
All faithful, true, and generous, and kind—
As friends should be, of kindred heart and mind—
Albeit, even, if these eyes to beauty's charms were
    blind.

TO E.

WHILE thou art, dear, so young, beware
With whom thy tender love to share:
Do not, sweet girl, thy smiles bestow
On one unworthy; for the bow
Of Cupid, oft flings poison'd darts
To ruin unsuspecting hearts:
Though this life may not blend with thine,
Thou art my choicest Valentine,

TO S.

COME, once more, to Love's shrine;
Your snow-white arms entwine,
Close clinging as the vine,
And whispering "I am thine—
Thine, dearest,—ever thine!"

WHEN DORA DIED.

DREARY, dreary,
Fundy's mists are sweeping
Up the stricken vales of Westmoreland:
Weary, weary
Is my heart and weeping,
While the cold waves dash upon the strand.

Fillèd, fillèd
Is the land with sorrow,
In loud wailing roars the angry sea:
Stillèd, stillèd
Will they be to-morrow—
Summer-notes, and murmurs on the lea.

Falling, falling
Are the leaves in light showers,
Crimson as the Rhine-land, in whose marts,

Calling, calling
Thousands are the night-hours—
Heaven for mercy on their orphan'd hearts.

Faded, faded
Summer flowers are lying
In the hectic groves, and meadows scre :
Jaded, jaded
Northern flocks are flying
Southward, high above the sedgy mere.

Fletting, fletting
Are the later swallows
On like journey where the frost-dews lay
Wetting, wetting
All the mossy hollows,
And the upland pastures by the Bay.

Glowing, glowing
In the west this even
Are the cloud-rifts, shimmering as the light :
Flowing, flowing
Through the gates of Heaven,
When the day-dawn lifts the veil of Night.

Coldly, coldly
Blent with autumn-mists lie
Eve's dark shadows 'pon the hills away ;

Boldly, boldly
Like a giant sentry,
Chapeau Dieu keeps vigil o'er the Bay.

Wildly, wildly,
Midnight-winds are blowing,
Icy-chill, across the maple hills :
Mildly, mildly
Though the stars are glowing,
Deep commotion all this bosom fills.

Gleaming, gleaming,
Is the seaward light'ning
Which the dark skirts of the south illume ;
Beaming, beaming
As a fancy bright'ning
Soul of poet in the midst of gloom.

Breaking, breaking
Is the east-dawn, shining
As the Cynthia through a leaden cloud ;
Making, making
A fair amber lining—
Weaving night a golden-belted shroud.

Lay me, lay me,
While the world is waking,
Down to dream on what has gone before ;

Pray ye, pray ye
Lest my heart be breaking,
God to bring her to my side once more.

Wake me, wake me
Out of this soul-gloom, when
The kind sun has dried all earth's tears sad ;
Take me, take me
To my darling's tomb, then
I, too, shall cease weeping—and be glad.

ELEGIES.

IN MEMORIAM.

E. R. P. H.

SAD and low,
Sad and low,
Over the hills of snow,
Winds of the dying day moan from the sea ; .
Fast fall the shades of night ;
While from the stars of light
Angels speed, guarding her now tenderly.

Softly tread,
Softly tread,
Baby is lying dead,

Fair, calm and pure, as a cherub asleep.
Neither the icy breath,
Nor the pale hand of death
Blasts the flowers angels watch over and keep

Latest one,
Latest one
Blossom'd 'neath autumn's sun,
White rose, and lily, in one essence blent;
Winds of the winter wild,
Chilling the darling child,
Only restored again what Heaven lent.

IN MEMORIAM.

E. R. C

DEAD! the winds are lying,
And my heart is sighing,
While the day is dying
At the golden portals of the West:
Shadows of the night fall
O'er the land, and sea all;
As their voices soft call
To me, from the mansions of the blest.

Dead ! the hopes and pleasures,
And beloved treasures—
Filling all my measures,
With, alas ! the story of my grief:
Idols I was keeping
In my home, lie sleeping ;
Though, restores not weeping,
A lost one, lain low as an autumn leaf.

Yet with prayer and praises
Blent, to Heaven it raises
The heart from earth, through mazes
Of dark sin guiding oft the famish'd soul
To the sacred rivers,
Where the Angel-givers
Make us, ever, livers
With them, as the years eternal roll.

Still, night-shades are falling,
Still I hear them calling—
My lost darlings calling—
For their Mother, from the darkening West :
Following one another ;
Leading, now, each other ;
Lo ! they lead their Mother
Through the shadows to the land of rest.

THE DEATH OF EMMA.

SLOWLY, slowly,
Sable shades are falling
Down the crimson portals of the west :
Lowly, lowly
Orphan hearts are calling
For their mother ere they went to rest.

Sadly, sadly,
April winds were wailing,
Darkness reigned, where all before was light
Madly, madly
Stricken hearts were ailing,
Through the long, long dreary hours of night.

Faintly; faintly
Shone the stars of Heaven
Through the gloomy, cold, and misty sky ;
Saintly, saintly,
Fillèd with the leaven—
That last look-of Immortality.

Praising, praising,
Though we might not hear it,
Were the angels on the morrow morn ;
Raising, raising
Up the blessed spirit
Of her body, wearied, faint, and worn,

IN MEMORIAM.

A Dirge.

At the "Morgue," in New York, was brought in the apparel of some unfortunate female, which alone remained for identification ; and, upon which were written some beautiful lines entitled "Only the Clothes that She Wore." These stanzas are penned in memory of the author of that poem, who died under melancholy circumstances shortly after its publication.

TOLL'D the bell for the dead :
Toll'd the bell solemnly ! No more his lyre shall be
Tuned ; in silent gloom, sleeps he within the tomb ;
Mourn him then—o'er his bed

Strew the sad cypress leaves !
Heard ye that song he sang—how its soft echoes rang
All o'er the Continent, tender as a lament !
For him this spirit grieves.

Though for him others here,
Father or mother dear, sister or lover near—
Have a far higher right, still there is love and might
Within the wider sphere

Of a world's sympathy !
Was his life's " history " like hers a " mystery,"
As *hers*, too, without a friend, who might rejoice to lend
Aid, ere the soul should flee.

Was his heart torn with woe—
Hopeless; in clouds of care, driven to mad despair,
Like a dark tempest-night 'reft of the star of light
    Glooming o'er all below.

Hark ! through the even air
Hear the wild agony of a soul born to be
Heart-full of melody.   List ! as through space they
    flee—
    Wilder notes of despair.

Was there no succour nigh
Was there no hand to save, generous, kind and brave?
Was there no sympathy *then* to soothe tenderly ?
    Was there no power on high

To save, ere he should die ?
As the cold dews of death, as the faint hurried breath,
Laid him low 'neath the sod, hurried his soul to God,
    Heard ye not his loud cry ?

Ye angels bright, above,
Heard and forgot the past, mayhap around him cast
Mercies—in hymnings soft, bearing his soul aloft—
    Bearing on wings of love.

In this all sinful sphere—
On the swift tide of life, amid the woe, the strife,

And the vain fleeting joy, like any poet-boy,
    He had but sinnèd here.

    Low-stricken with the rod,
Let *one* this tribute bring—a humble offering,
Although he knew thee ne'er, a poet's heart can
    share,—
    " Saved by the will of God"

    Wert thou ?—though we but know
That thou art with the dead, that we our tears may
    shed.
For thee whose life did flow, in that sad tale of woe,—
    Hope whispers " *even so*."

SONGS OF IMMORTALITY.

THE NATIVITY.

O'ER the winter-wold
    Clouds of gold
Clustered neath the shadows in the West :
    Lo ! a lovely star,
    From afar,
Lonely twinkled on the azure breast
Of evening, for the day had gone to rest.

    Glorious as a sun,
    One by one,
Other orbs then glinted beams of light :
    Sparkling as the stones
    'Pon the thrones
Of Angels, whose fair wings of snowy white
Clave the blue ether all that hallow'd night.

Swift as meteors fly
Thwart the sky,
Angel and Seraph on like errand bent :
Through the frosty air,
Flashing fair,
See downy plumes with iris-hues besprent,
That to each other added glory lent.

In the realms of air,
Everywhere,
The blue-eyed Cherubs hover to and fro :
Softly they alight
As flakes white
In winter-tide, what time the East winds blow,
And sport and circle o'er the waste of snow.

'Pon the ethereal plain
Look ! amain,
The humble host, in serried order, prone :
Far as eye can gaze,
Through the haze
Of distant Heaven, round a jasper throne,
Wheeling : aloft, the Dove Almighty shone.

Lo ! descending flee
Suddenly—
By Satan led, who as a bolt is hurl'd—

J

Thick as locust-flights—
Damnèd Sprites!
Hell for an instant shadow'd the fair world,
While all her Powers were down to Tart'rus whirl'd!

Lost, in tempest-rack,
Frowning, black!—
A million shades, then, veil th' hallowed sight,
Covering land and sea,
Momently—
Earth, air, sky thunder'd, flashing tongues of light—
The powers accurst meet, rush in wretched plight.

Saw ye, from the North,
Issue forth
In rolling waves the pulsing prism light?
Behold the Aurora-beams
In swift gleams
Illume the skirts from pole to pole of Night,
Whose lamps undimmed flash through the glory
[bright;
And the meteor fair
In mid-air,
Swiftly darting as the lightning flies—
Circling left and right
Startlings bright,
Those joyous, happy children of the skies,
That dance and play to Angel's melodies.

Heard ye bleatings low
On the snow ?
Saw ye flocks about their keepers prest ?
Hush'd—nor sound—nor sigh—
Earth and sky,
From North to South, from East to farthest West,
Were, until harp'd, the Harpers of the blest.

And the Crown sublime,
In full prime,
O'erarching all—God's bow across the sky :
List ! ten thousand quires
Strike their lyres,
And anthems loud ascend from Earth, on High,
Where star to star repeats the melody.

As a sphere of light,
Glancing bright,
Th' Archangel descried ye from above :
Hail ! Hail ! " All is well,"
Gabriel
Sang, in a voice thrill'd with celestial love,
Beneath the glory of that radiant Dove.

Hark ! their harps they tune,
As the moon
Treads majestic up the Eastern hills :

Like a noble Queen
Fair in sheen,
She trips the skies : awhile, in joyous trills,
That voice angelic yet the night air fills.

What glad tidings brings
He, and sings
To the shepherds on the plains below ;
Whose entrancèd ears
Blent with fears,
The holy news received, as on the snow
They knelt, encircled in a heavenly glow.

And, while hovering there,
Myriads were,
They still with wonder shook : increasing more
And more, till Cherubim
And Seraphim
The tale retold, from whose sweet lips did pour
Mercy and love, abiding evermore.

Through the valleys fair
Everywhere
Those twin-words flowed, as streamlets down a vale :
Far across the main
Rang again
The echoes unto other lands, where hail
A thousand hearts, to-day, the joyous tale.

" Unto you is born !"
Lo ! is born ! !
To you, and all the world, a Saviour given :
Star of Bethlehem's morn !
Whose light, when all the clouds are riven,
Shall guide you safely through the gates of Heaven.

" Glory to God," they sang,
Notes that rang
From Heaven's centre to the depths of hell !
" In the highest ;". fair,
Everywhere !
Peace, " Peace on Earth"—for evermore to dwell,
And " Good will toward men," hail ! all is well !

Look ! a wondrous sight !
With delight,
And fearless awe, the herdsmen are elate :
To eyes upturned appear
In the clear
· Dawn, legions winging through the golden gate
Of Eastern heaven, in majestic state.

O'er the wintry waste
The shepherds haste
With Gabriel, who fresh tidings glad convey'd :
The star of Bethlehem
Luring them,

Whose beams on Him, in lonely manger, play'd—
The Saviour babe, in swaddling bands arrayed.

O'er the wintry wild,
To the child
Were led the " wise men " by that glowing sign,
Bringing, as was meet,
Offerings sweet
To Him, late born beside the stalls of kine—
Of David's house foretold, the Royal Babe divine.

Hail! tender form of one,
The Triune Son,
The Saviour mild, upon His mother's breast :
Daylight eclips'd was dim,
While over Him
Stood that bright Star—that Angel's glowing crest,
Blent with the halo round the Virgin blest.

Oh, love most infinite !
Rapt'rous sight !
The lowliness and glory of the scene :
Oh, mercy past compare,
All may share—
The living, dying, and all that have been !
Upon whose breast sin-wearied *all* may lean.

IMMORTALITY.

PART FIRST.

OH, Thou, Who hast been ever, and shall be
For evermore Immortal, touch this lyre,
And fill this spirit with poetic fire,
To sing these lays of Immortality :
But should the flame be quenchèd ere my song
Shall have been finished, yet from out the coal,
And ashes dead, may some sparks upward fly,
Re-kindled by Thy quick'ning breath on high,
Amid the choirs of angelic souls ;
Or should the path be perilous and long
Here, in life's journey, o'er the toilsome way ;
Or I wax faint and weary, let me pray
To Thee for ample strength : Lord, with Thy light
Guide me, and all who love Thy name, through sin's
dark maze, aright.

As sunbeam to the shadow on the wall ;
As light to darkness in the etherial space ;
As life to death, are linked in close embrace
The spirit, and the body : But, o'er all
The God-imag'd of this fair universe,

Is spread the light of one grand truth, afar—
  That shines above the deep, dark-misted curse
Of sin, as brilliant as a southern star
Above the storm-cloud's skirt: Our bodies are
  Rest-mansions only on the shores of time—
Built of, and rotting back again to dust—
For souls immortal, while in faith-born trust
  They journey toward eternity: Sublime
The thought that all in love are called to join the
    angelic-just.

As incense rising from the meads of June;
  As ocean-mists unto their native skies;
  As the soul-stirring earth-sung melodies
That lift to heaven, blended in one tune,
  So rise our prayer-born yearnings, and on high
The angels chant the grand mysterious theme,
  In strains befitting Immortality!
Oft do we see them in still, trancèd dream,
  Like to the glory in the east away,
  When Phœbus bursts the golden gates of day!
Shine round our hearths in halo-circl'd beam,
  Ye spirit-guides! Come, point the morning
    way—
Doubts, fears dispel, and every cloud of sorrow—
Where the dawn, all orbs of light shall quench, of
    God's eternal morrow,

There is a life in every germèd thing,
  A spark immortal that can never die;
  Death's messengers across the wide world fly,
And, everywhere, the poisoned arrows fling
  Into the hearts of leaf, and plant, and flower—
Aye, man and beast—yet do they not flash out,
  And cease forever. The Almighty power
  That binds the electric forces, every hour
But changes the vitality throughout
  The leaven'd whole, evolving germ from germ :
  The eternal Chymist who hath made the worm,
Created man; albeit, from the rust
  Long gathered in the womb of ages, Learn.
Life's a grand chain, whose links unite the atomies
  of dust !

God's wondrous works around the cyclic span
  Of far-off ages, beyond farthest time,
  Shall be eternal as they've been sublime :
Nature is but the archetype of man,
  Convuls'd and changing as the human heart ;
With cloud and sunshine on her brow, by turns ;
  With calm and tempest, forming there a part
Of her existence : in her bosom burns
  The self-same lamp of Immortality ;
  As leaf from branch ; as acorn from the tree ;
As flower from the parent stem, are we

A part of her—aye, from her loins were cast—
  Like to a mother's, we cling tenderly
Unto her side ; and, even in death, sleep on her breast
  at last.

All nature weeps, for over the fair land
  Death's icy fingers have been spread, alas !
  All nature weeps, for every blade of grass,
And leaf, and flower—from great Ocean's strand
  Far back to groves behind the ancient hills—
Low-stricken lie upon the heart of earth.
  No longer now the voice of Summer fills
The welkin with her clear harmonious mirth.
  Lo, Winter ! snow-crown'd, from the wild north
    skies
    The storm-king comes—swift as an eagle flies,
    By fierce gales borne—and, like a great sea-wall,
    Dark rolling clouds, black as a funeral pall,
Enwrap his form : Hark ! from the mountains he
The death-curse shouts, till echoes back Spring Im
    mortality !

Though nature mourn'd ; and, stirr'd with wailings
    loud
  The autumn winds swept over land and sea ;
  Though nature mourn'd, peaceful and silently
Earth lies asleep, now, 'neath her snowy shroud.

No more the heavens weep in frequent showers,
Commingling with her dew-born tears below;
No more the stars the long, long, sad night-hours
Through gloomy mists, and dark fogs, faintly glow.
The skies are clear, oft, as in summer's prime;
And morn and eve are lovely to behold,
As they trip through, at their appointed time,
In east or west the sun-glint gates of gold—
Whence spring shall step, from o'er the crystal sea,
Type of the resurrection, and of immortality.

May war soon cease to desolate the earth;
And truth, and love, and charity but dwell
In the abodes of men; and star-born Mirth
Cheer her sad sister Sorrow with the spell
Of her all-pitying tenderness; and peace,
On dove-white wings, descend from heaven again:
Hail, blessed hour! From the azure main
Shall Seraphs come the prisoners to release;
With balm for each sin-struck, immortal soul,
Stamped with the seal of faith: Then shall the
roll
Of angel-anthems fill the startled world;
The harvest shall be gathered; and the cry
Of souls repentant shall ascend on high
The mercy-seat; while sin and death are down to
Tart'rus hurl'd.

No more the land the voice of summer fills ;
  And, through the shadows of the dying day,
  The northern flocks pursue their airy way,
And homeward speed beyond the southern hills ;
No more are heard the sweet, melodious trills
  Of tender birds that cannot longer stay
To bear the frost-dews and the fever chills
  Of autumn time, that will by morrow lay
Low, low the leaves, and lovely flower in death :
But, why lament ? Shall not the quick'ning breath
  Some future springtide visit all again ;
  And every link throb in the pulsing chain
Of life, aye never, nevermore to die,
Transfigured in the glorious light of Immortality !

Dear Summer's dying : on her emerald crest
  The dark streak'd stains of swift-returning dust
  Are mingled with the brown and yellow rust
Of those green tresses, late. From east to west,
From north to south, upon her fated breast,
  The hectic glow is mingled with the must
  Of dead leaves, dropping from her sylvan bust,
Soon 'neath the snows, in scattered heaps, to rest.
Dear Summer's dying ; while the sad skies pour
  Down floods of tears that to the solemn sea
In rivers flow, across the stricken earth ;
Alas, alas, she is, she is no more !

Hush'd, cold, and lifeless, now her heart of glee—
Not death, but sleep! where faith awaits a grand,
    immortal birth.

Dear Summer's dead! oh, hearken to the wail
    Of sighing winds, and to the dying lay
    Of her last swan. Lo! clouds of ashy grey
Her fair face covering, as a mourning veil :
List to the north-blasts sobbing down the dale,
    Where swallows fletted only yesterday :
    See clamorous geese, across the stormy bay
Now speeding, homeward, swift before the gale.
Dear Summer's dead! but shall revive again ;
    Albeit, in the glory of the Sun—
Her bosom decked with sweetest, fairest flowers,
And greenest leaves, begemm'd in purest rain ;
    And her sweet quires returnèd every one—\
Immortalized: no more to die: her destiny and ours.

Shall ever end these days of drear unrest ;
    Shall ever cease this life of striving vain ;
    Shall ever come back to the mind again
But the remembrance of joys, doubly blest—
    Of bye-gone hours of childhood's innocence :
When the meridian of our years is past,
    How we do feel all with a keener sense—
The trials and temptations ; the fierce blast

Of sin, whose alloy is earth-suffering—
Although immortal, we yet madly cling
To the false world; but, guide us Lord aright,
And fill our hearts with holy love and fear;
In living, and in dying, be Thou near,
And the dark mists of sin dispel with Thine immor-
tal light.

What breast could bear the never ending grief;
What eyes could weep the ever falling tears;
What life survive the slowly torturing years
Of helpless, hopeless sorrow; oh! how brief
Would be existence, if our loves of Earth
Should have an end within the cold, dark grave.
The hearts that joy'd upon us at our birth;
The dear ones severed by the wide, wild sea;
The friends of youth we loved so tenderly;
The parent, brother, sister—the good, brave
Heart that adored us till the latest breath,
But now asleep upon the bed of death—
All were inspired with that faith, God-given,
That we, and they, immortal were, might meet again
in Heaven.

Across the hills of Time, and down the vales,
We wander oft, as stray'd sheep from the cote;
And, on Life's ocean tempest tost we float
As helmless barges, with rent and shattered sails,

Beneath dark skies, wind-swept by fiercest gales ;
  Nor sun, nor star, to guide us on our way :
  To reach a haven of rest, from day to day
We struggle on ; but helpless, nought avails,
  Save, when bereft, we raise our eyes on high
  In earnest prayer : Lo! out of the clear'd sky
The star of Faith, now, as a moon full grown,
  Beams with the light of Immortality,
  And sheds its rays far over land and sea.
God made us not mere "atoms," "leaves" to be by
  time-winds strewn.

Dark, angry clouds may sweep and rush along
  The boundless skies ; and fire-spear'd lightnings
    glow ;
  And thunders crash upon the world below ;
And tempest-winds roll madly, fierce and strong,
  The mighty wave 'pon every ocean-shore ;
  And earthquakes all the rocks and mountains rend
Of Earth's foundations ; and the heavens pour
  Down sulph'rous flames, where fire and brimstone
    blend,
  'Pon the wreck of ages! Yet nor tempest grand,
Nor the spear'd lightning, nor the awful crash
Of thunder, and of earthquake ; nor the dash
  Of mighty billows on the ocean-strand ;
Nor the fire-torrent, burning earth and sea,
Can e'en one of God's heirs destroy, of Immortality !

So softly tread the star-lit plains of space,
  Freed from the bondage of this earth-born life—
  The trial, sorrow, and the warring strife
Of passion—where sin-demons madly chase
  Us, till we fall faint, gasping, aye, for breath:
So swiftly speed, on spirit-wings of light,
  Far up beyond the night-dark vales of death,
With angel-guides to helm our course aright,
  All through the ages of eternity;
  E'en this alone were joy most heavenly
For souls immortal: But, when add to this,
  To those who love Him, here, with all their heart,
  God's promise, which His holy words impart,
Eye hath not seen, nor mind conceivèd, such trans-
      cendant bliss.

Childlike, we gambol on the stormy strand
  Of Time; with idle toys around us strewn,
  Of earthly hope and pleasure, as are thrown
By the wild, wind-swept billows, weed and sand,
  In scattered heaps, upon the ocean's shore:
We are, too, only children on this sphere,
In the beginning of existence, here,
  For we were made to live for evermore!
From the creation to the end of Man
  Will have been scarce a year, a day, an hour,
Compared to that neve-rending span

Of life eternal : The same mighty Power,
Who chaos germ'd, and sunn'd the dark with light,
Made all immortal as the stars, that deck His throne
    to-night !

To struggle on, unknown, uncared for, here—
    Albeit, yearning oft to interchange
    The sweets of friendship, and compelled to range,
From day to day, and live within a sphere,
    Where is no love, no tender sympathy :
    To lonely wander o'er the roughen'd sea,
Like a lost pilgrim 'pon a desert wild,
Or in some dark lane a deserted child,
    What boots it ?   We cannot forsaken be
    When angel-guides attend us constantly :
" Though toss'd about, as sea-weed round the rocks,
    Upon Life's billows, wounded by the shocks
Of harsher natures—faint not, patient be ;
Thou art Immortal, and thy home's beyond the azure
    sea."

The cold, sleet winds of yesterday, that swept
    Their icy showers across the shivering Earth,
Have passed away. The northern winds have slept,
    Till this calm winter noon-hour, since the birth
Of early morn ; and, oh ! how beauteously
The same blue dome o'ereaches land and sea,

K

As bright and glorious as in Summer-tide ;
The same fair orb too, shines afar and wide
Across the vales : Lo ! every forest tree
   Bows down its silver branches 'neath the skies—
   Now flashing, beaming, sparkling with the dyes
   Of myriads of ice-prisms, wherein lies
A world of light ! What must the glory be
Of Earth, clothed in her Summer robes of Immor-
      tality.

All that is carnal with the body dies ;
   And, from this rotting prison-house of clay,
   The soul must yet escape and flee away,
On spirit-wings to the Eternal skies,
   For we are made Immortal : Life on Earth
Is but the reflection of a higher state :
   Though Faith, and Prayer, and holy Praise give
         birth
   To joys celestial, and of untold worth,
Our noblest aspirations must await
   Their grand fulfilment in futurity :
Hearts that are hallow'd—tender, pure, and great
   With dyes of Love and Mercy—here shall be
Accepted only after they have died,
And risen as morn-mists to Heaven, there to be
      glorified !

The lamps are all out in the wild, wan sky,
  As Phœbus rises, from a throne of gold,
Above the pale and misty folds that lie
  In one great sea, upon the wood and wold !
'Tis morning ! Lo, the fog-clouds speed away,
As Ghosts of Night, across the steaming bay,
  By north winds borne: upon the valley's floor
The sunlight sparkles : every forest tree
Shines iris-hued, in thick frost drapery,
  From yonder hills down to the wintry shore.
List! sweet as song-birds, squirrels merrily
Chirp in the snow-clad evergreens. Ah, me !
  Why should we e'er weep for the days of yore—
Winter but types the Summer-time to come,
                    " Forevermore."

Beneath the lesser glories of the night,
  Lo ! Sirius flashes in the winter sky ;
  And swiftly as the twinkling of an eye,
He shines, alternate; now in emerald light,
In red, in sapphire ; now in purest white :
  The world is steept in slumber; verily
  Peace reigns, and drowsy mists float dreamily
'Pon the cold hills, as Trivia, silver-bright,
Treads her starr'd courts of Heaven: everywhere,
  The glory of God's countless realms above,
The glory of His earth below, and sea—

All clearly mirror'd in the moonlit air,
  Stampt with His seal of ever-enduring love—
Foreshadows our grand heritage of immortality.

Orion's belt, in ether-fields afar,
  Shines triple-fold upon the azure sea,
  'Mid constellations grand : the canopy
Of his high throne, lo! sister orbs instar ;
While round about him lesser spheres there are,
  All beautiful, and glowing splendidly,
  Down through the moonless winter-night: oh, see
Them rivalling now Aurora's throbbing bar—
The Pleiades and Hyades above ;
  The " Mighty Hunter," amid clusters fair ;
Majestic Sirius, flashing bright, below ;
The " Bull," the " Dogs " performing works of love ;
  Amid them, too, behold the gentle " Hare"—
Mysterious, grand, immortal! blent in one harmoni-
    ous glow.

The sun is down, and through the ebon shades
  The night-lamps faintly flicker in the sky ;
  And cold and leaden mists are sailing by
The western hills, across the river-glades,
  While earth lies sleeping 'neath her snowy shroud
  And Cynthia rises from her throne—a cloud
Of silver-mist—into the silent blue :

Lo! suddenly a form of emerald hue,
With star-lit angel-wings and flashing feet,
Floats, hov'ring in mid air; and, oh, how sweet
  The scent of everlasting flowers that twine
  Around her crest; how soft the rays that shine
Upon her brow, reflecting Heaven's light,
Where " Evermore " is writ and stampt in golden
    letters bright.

As countless as the pebbles of the stream,
  Or as the grains of sand upon the shore,
  The star-flakes sparkle on the frosty floor
Of yonder valley : in a golden gleam
  The hoar-mists quiver 'neath the early sun ;
And where the hills are clothed in mantles white,
  Festoonèd gracefully the branches dun
Of the fir-copses glitter, too, in light :
  Clear, fresh and bracing is the young moon's breath,
Pure as a maiden's : 'neath the fairest skies,
Lo, all the land in shimmering beauty lies :
  Such glory upon earth, asleep in death,
Is of that greater glory type, when we
Die, and put on the snow-white robes of Immortality.

Awake, arouse ye from the sleep of sin !
  Behold the dawning of a brighter day,
  Where Beth'lem's Star hath lighted up the way
That leads to glory : only enter in

With steps of faith, and thou shalt surely win
   Th' Immortal Crown that shall be thine for aye :
Oh, Father, let us from this hour begin
   To love and fear Thee, and when led astray
By the false tempter, lift our hearts to Thee
In earnest prayer : good Lord, our guardian be :
   Hail ! blest return of hallow'd Christmas-tide,
That sent a Saviour for the world, lost long.
   Oh, come ! and join the anthems, far and wide,
That angels sing through Heaven to-night, in praises
     loud and strong.

Come back again ! ye hallowed hours of youth,
   With faith, and hope, and star-eyed innocence ;
   Come back again, and loose the heart-strings, tense
With years of by-gone sinfulness and ruth ;
Come, heal the anguish with thy balmy sooth—
   Dispel the mists that pall the stricken sense,
   Before we may be called away from hence—
Fresh from the fountain of Eternal Truth.
   Away, then, Sorrow !   Ever-during Joy
Is the sure lot of each prayer-guided soul,
   Re-quickened by the All-creative breath,
   In Zion's mansions ; where the sweet alloy
Of angel-love shall blend with the soft roll
Of angel harpings, far beyond the night-black gates
     of Death.

THE STORY OF SYLVALLA.

The scene of this poem, which, when completed, will embrace some five or six cantos— is laid by a lake near the Carman river (in the County of Westmoreland, N.B), that, flowing through swamp and plain, finds its way into the Washadermoak river—the waters of which latter, after pouring through a lake of the like name, blend with those of the "St. John."

AMID the maple groves,
And grazing hills, and grassèd intervales
Of "Petcoowak," fanned by the southern gales
Of Fundy's Bay, these sylvan notes I've sung:
Albeit, but faint echoes that have rung
    Upon the harp Divine
    Of Nature, as what time
She dons the emerald robes of joyous spring
And gladsome summer: timorous I bring
    These first-fruits from a lyre

Unskill'd, with no desire
Beyond a lowly wish that some stray note
May gently drop on life's rough sea, and float
Its sympathy unto an ailing heart—
And, of its burdens sharing there a part—
As a cloud-shade its crest
On ocean's troubled breast ;
As angel songs, on mercy's errand bent,
In simple trust of prayer and faith,
These humble lays are sent.

THE STORY OF SYLVALLA.

CANTO 1ST.

How long and drear the hours
Since yestermorn, how full this heart of care ;
And, if these eyes have wept, yet dire despair
Shall not o'erwhelm my soul,
Though full the bitter bowl
Already ! aye, this dark tempestuous night
Shall nerve my soul before to-morrow's light,
With fresh resolves, shall burst
These galling chains accursed !
Far from this dark reality I'll fly for visions bright.

From persecution freed,
I'll roam the earth to find a solitude
Where lives the red man in the deep wild wood;
    But still not all alone
    To dwell, for thou my own,
My dear Sylvalla, shall I take to grace this forest
    home.

    He said, and bade adieu
To Scotia's shores, and with his Indian bride
Young Rodlyn journeyed. 'Twas the summer-
    tide.
    The happy, hopeful pair,
    Nerv'd by the bracing air
Of Fundy, hasten o'er the boisterous bay;
Bright was the morn, the earliest of May.
    Both wield the pliant oar,
    And " Ouangonda's " shore
Reach, as the night shades veil the crimson west,
Where, wearied, beside the " Falls " they lie them
    down to rest.

    The tumbling current sweeps
By their wide tent of red-deer skins undrest,
Stretch'd 'twixt twin lime rocks, on the river's
    breast.
    The moon shines soft and fair,

As they lie sleeping there,
Beneath whose beams the foaming waters play
And gambol, while the silver-tippèd spray
Is driven by the western breeze across the rock-
    wall'd way.

'Tis Morn! through golden mist
The rising orb ascends the eastern hills,
And streams his glory everywhere, and fills
With beauty, love, and life the Summer-earth :
Dear June is breathing incense ; in great mirth
    The song-stirr'd hills rejoice,
    As in harmonious voice ;
The air, the water, and the glowing brow
Of yonder wood blend their soft echoes now,
    And 'mid the glad'ning scene,
    Upon the waving sheen,
The couple guide their bark canoe, and swift the
    waters plough.

First, through those rocky walls
That guard the river, they pursue their way.
And by noontide pass over the " Grand Bay,"
    And evening touch " Long Reach,"
    Upon whose western beach,
Beneath a shade of stately elm-trees,—
That tremble, shimmering in the western breeze,

Where late a passing shower
Swept by at sunset hour—
On cool and mossy couch they calm repose,
Lulled by the river's current, till the dawn is flush'd
      with rose.

      Anon by sloping hill,
By elmy grove, and gràssèd intervale,
And islets green, with southern breeze they sail
      Swift and right gracefully,
      Full-joyous, happy, free
As the wild wind that wafts them ; as the song
Of summer birds that cheer them all day long ;
      Close by the river's side
      The happy couple glide :
Hark ! the gay squirrels cherrup, merrily,
Within the copses of the green fir tree ;
Through whose dun branches flicker, now, the sun-
      beams smilingly.

      While bright the star of day
Wheel'd up the east, and flashèd on " Bellisle,'
The light canoe sped on toward " Long Isle,"
      Apast whose dexter shore
      They hasten, swift as oar
      And favouring breeze can take
      Them to the glassy lake

Of " Wash 'demoak,"--on whose glowing breast,
While slowly fall eve's shades, the lovers lay them
   down to rest.

     That night was mild, serene,
And beautiful, as they together slept
In their birch-couch, while the warm zephyrs
   stept—
     As trips wool-footed hare
     On white snow fleecy-fair—
Across the moonlit waters, whispering:
List! Through those balmy hours the echoing
Of far faint night-calls from the maple hills
Blend with the purling of shower-swollen rills,
     That, swift as running steeds,
     Haste down the June-flower'd meads,--
Sweet, violet-scented—perfuming the air—
Sky, moon, stars, moods are all reflected there,
     Clear as a lover's dream,
     Upon the drowsy stream
Whose wavelets kiss the shell, in lullaby,
Soft as the gentle murmuring roll of a calm sum-
   mer-sea.

     Another day dawn'd fair,
And joyously the couple paddled, slow
The river, like named as the lake below;

Far up through mossy swales,
Past groves, and intervales,
To where the red men track,
From the " Wash' de moak
To Canaan's stream, the moose and cariboo,
O'er wild moor-lands—untrodden but by few
White men of sporting fame,
In quest of health and game.
Both faint and weary, camp upon a plain,
Beside the river—on moss'd couch how smooth the
night-hours wane.

Rehearsing everywhere
Is Nature the old taste of summer-love :
' Mid stretches bright of silver-birchen grove,
And pale green beechen wood
That have for ages stood
The lightning's arrow and the tempest's blast,
They journey on where lo the fir trees cast
A gloomier shade of green,
Across the forest seen,
Like evil portents ; or across love's sky,
Dark ominous clouds. " Oh, hark :—
Did you not heed a bark,
Or wild whoop, Rodlyn ? Soft—do you not hear ?
Bend down and silently incline thine ear
To the canoe's side." " No, Sylvalla, no !

'Tis but the echo of wild sounds below—
Some wolf or fox whose howlings far and wide,
In woods like these and forest-depths, are heard at
    even-tide."

        Beneath the western rim
The orb is sinking, while a blaze of light
Illumes the skirt of fast descending night,
        And flushes fold on fold
        Of cloudlets manifold.
A crimson smile that gently melts away,
O'erspreads the visage of expiring day,
        Reflecting as a dream
        The river in a gleam
So pale, so faint, so dim, and so like death
That one can almost feel the icy breath
In the chill wind that shoots the waters fleet ;
Can almost see the ghost-like winding sheet
        In the vapour that weaves
        Itself into the leaves,
And flowers and mosses upon either bank,
As up the reaches of the stream, the fog sweeps cold
    and dank.

        Thick from the waters rise
The steamy mists that softly woo the breeze,
And, later still, unto the trembling trees

In drowsy languor cling
Sylvalla's listening
For a recurrence of those noises dread ;
Absorbed in this remain unnoticèd
The solemn beauties of the early night,
And the great moon just rising on her right :
"Hark ! Rodlyn—down the stream ;
Aha, it is no dream ! "
"Speed on ! speed on in haste,
There is no time to waste !
They're close upon us," Rodlyn cries—" God knows
how long they've chased ! "·

They blend their mutual strength—
Sylvalla's arm was practised long ago,
And nature gave them courage.   On they go !
With hasty, sparkling drip,
The pliant blades scarce tip
The awakened currents. Through the forest far
Re-echo yells more loud than whoop of war
From the wild painted crew !
Quick, Rodlyn his canoe
Turned sharp about, while his brave bride shot down
the foremost two.

Withdrawing from its sheath
The keen-edged knife, he sprang across the prow

And dealt with certain death, the fatal blow
    On th' others, three, save one,
    Who from his bow now flung
An arrow, which thrice quickly Rodlyn's arm
Then caught, as raised to guard his bride from
    harm.
    She dashed the bladed oar—
    Ere scarce the deed was o'er—
Down on that savage head—it laid beside the bleed-
    ing four !

    This done, Sylvalla then
Lost not a moment, but in trembling haste
Drew out the poison with young lips as chaste,
    And pure as was her love.
    Come ! Rodlyn, let us move
    Our bark to yonder shore,
    We will not journey more
To-day—all tenderly she bound his wound,
And soothed with gentle ministerings—and all was
    love around.

    Lies hushed the breath of Heaven ;
And sullenly the river moves along ;
And solemnly the woods reflected throng
    The slumbering shore : afar,
    Faint beams the morning star,

And forest echoes shake the silent air :
From natural slumber, myriads, everywhere,
    Lift thankful hearts above,
    In pure harmonious love :
'Tis' morn! and oh! amid the scene, I feel my spirit
    move.

    Slow falls the western even,
Like an illumined chariot wheel diverge
The blushing beams, that still from day emerge,
And, lingering, court the soft and silent night,
As loth to part ; while far along the right
    Jet darkness, stooping, spreads
    Her skirt, ere Cynthia treads
Slow up the hills, that late with music rang,
To chambers grand on high—where now her robes
    bespangled hang.

    Like too, a heavenly form—
Majestic moves this fairy queen arrayed
In jewelled garb, long since in Heaven made,
Rock, mountain, wood, and ocean are the scenes
That win her love ; as, downward on the beams
Of her bright eye, ten thousand beauties glide,
Enchanting earth, who welcomes her his fair celes-
    tial bride.

L

A vision to behold,
The summer-moon smiles through the crystal air,
On earth and sky like glory everywhere
From a celestial crown
Ten thousand gems shine down
And brightly sparkle through the crystal sheen!
The beauty and the glory of the scene
Are mirrored on the waters, all the night
The self-same influences bathe with light
The sleeping maple hills,
Whose faint, soft murmuring rills
Flow gently down to fir-copsed vales—hark! hear
the early trills.

Lo ! up the eastern woods
In crimson clad, and full of splendour, comes
The king of light.   The little feathered ones—
Athrough the deep wood—stir the faltering wind
With joy and song, and mutual greetings kind ;
And from the light canoe
The lovers bid adieu
To their nocturnal home,
Yet further on they roam
By hill and dale, through swamp and tangled
brake ;
Lo ! changed the scene—the journey s o'er—they've
reached the Canaan lake.

' Tis sweet to meet on earth
Earth's dearest friends, a-past long absent hours,
And to revisit those beloved bow'rs
Where true affection dwells—our childhood's
home,
' Tis sweet in memory to be alone
With those we love, whene'er 'mong strangers
thrown;
But sweeter far I ween
The pleasure that hath been
Bestowed on all who've realized some long-long cher-
ished dream.

Ambition truly then
Hath reached her goal. The hopes, the doubts,
the fears
Of all we wished for, prayed for most, appears
Concentered in one word,
That hour by hour had stirred,
With thrilling throbs, the very inmost heart
Of noble minds—it is a vital part,
Ambition! " ruling alike the court, camp, empire and
the mart."

Warm tears of gladness flow
From his dark eyes, as Rodlyn finds the dream
Now realized, so long the secret theme

Of his night visions—This the promised land
He yearned to reach; where Nature's lavish hand
    Bestows her rarest dowers
    On trees, and herbs, and flowers
That now perfume the breath of eve, as calmly speed
    the hours.

    Day's last faint murmurs have
Scarce died, and nought disturbs the dreamy
    hush,
Save now and then, within the tangled brush
Around the lake, some bird or startled hare ;
The wood-encircled mirror—oh ! how fair,
    Reflecting the deep hue
    Of Heaven's jewelled blue ;
Like diamonds in sapphire set—just as the moon
    rose there.

    Now to the light canoe,
From dreams refreshed the joyous couple hie.
'Tis morn's first breath, beneath as grand a sky
    As ever circled Heaven,
    Or to the earth was given.
Hark ! music sweetly trembles on the breeze,
And mingles with the warbling of the trees,
    The voice that there is heard—
    Melodious every word—

Vibrates through him, from her all glowing
 crest ;
Oh ! sympathy, how art thou doubly blest—
Oh ! what a freight of joy thou bearest along
On the deep, passionate, and mysterious song
  Of a pure woman's love ;
  Who hath not felt it move
A thousand thoughts ? whose echoes in the heart's
 heart-centre throng.

  They circuit round the lake,
As softly dips the smooth and pliant blade
That Rodlyn wields. Two months agone, he said,
  Our journeyings began ;
  Although but a short span
Of our young life, Sylvalla, heavenly joy
Hath been our lot, and, if we here employ
The hours aright, may still be full of love—
Oft let us lift our hearts to One above,
The All-wise, Good, and Merciful, even when cares
 annoy.

  He will be with us here,
Though far around the savage red man dwells,
Aye, even last night I heard some hideous yells
  Re-echo from yon hill.
  I felt a transient thrill

At first; why tremble ? fear not lovèd one—
I'll visit them before to-morrow's sun :
By gifts, and by kind offices, their hearts must first
    be won.

      Air, Earth, and Heaven are still ;
In the soft languor of the noon-tide sun
The wild flowers droop, and the wild songsters
    shun
The open plain, and seek the sheltering shade ;
Each busy life that had so lately made
      The morn to ring with joy,
      Now ceases to employ
The fleeting hours, but in a drowsy mood
Awaits the shadows of the western wood—
Soon mirrored on the smooth unrippled lake ;
List! music soft—the waters stir—the evening
    winds awake.

      Awake! awake, my love !
The amber streak across the Eastern sky
Hath shot, and Rodlyn, ere sunrise, must hie
      To yonder thicket, where
      The birch-fires stream the air
With light.   He moves in firm, yet cautious
    tramp,
And on approaching the first savage camp

He hears a wild halloo—
"Who comes! A friend or foe?"
The alarm is spread; the slumberers spring—each
    red man to his bow!

    "A friend, though stranger, comes
To offer presents from a distant land;
Who could not such a great and valiant band
    Of noblest warriors fear,
    Alone and helpless here,"
    Was Rodlyn's quick reply—
    Withdrawing from his thigh
A wampan belt. "Thrice welcome to my side,"
The Chieftain said,—"I know this well—'tis from
    a friendly tribe.

    "Ho! bring the calumet,
Tiouka! and the larder's best prepare;
Accept it, stranger, although humble fare,
    'Tis fresh—of yester's chase—
    The choicest of the race
That swept the plain; and brother let me fill
This bowl of friendship, for Oulissi's will
Is thine—whose heart flows full for thee, as yonder
    forest rill."

    "I thank thee, warrior—
But only came to ask protection where

My consort dwells, with me a life to share
In these dear wilds; we've only one week spent
Beside the lake, but in our birchen tent
    We hope long years to dwell
    In peace with thee.   Farewell
We bade, forever, to white friends behind
Three moons ago, yet, for thy greetings kind,
    But gratitude can say
    In feeble words to-day
Two hearts shall waft their thanks to thee on every
    morning wind.

    " And, as a trifling gift
Accept this box of beads, and pearls, and rings ;
The pearls are from a river, whose clear springs
    Beyond the mountains flow.
    'Twas there, long time ago,
A lovely maid, for him who came not, sighed
All through one moon, then laid her down and
    died !
    This was the chosen spot,
    But oh ! how sad their lot !
Where they so late had fondly pledged to meet,
The Indian boy sped on with hasty feet
    To kiss his Indian bride ;
    But, o'er a barren wide,
He missed the trail—alas ! when only dying reached
    her side.

" Aloud his spirit weeps!
Kimalla! oh! my loved one, art thou dead?
Too late! too late! let me support thy head:
    Ah, no! these dear dark eyes
    In eloquent replies
Look up to mine, as if instinct with life;
Speak! speak! my only loved one—speak, my
    wife!
    Her head is gently bent,
    As if in meek assent,
Then raised again, she smiles—she gasps a breath—
Her eye-balls swim—her eye-lids droop—her pale
    hands clasp in death.

" Aloud his spirit moans!
He gazed—and gazed—and wept—and gazed
    again
For hours, while night-winds whistled o'er the
    plain
    And through the neighbouring wood,
    In moanings loud he stood
Still gazing—still sustaining her dead form
Through the long night, and through the anxious
    morn
    In silence still he stood,
    And touched not aught of food—
How long, I know not but he fell, heart-broken,
    faint, and torn,

" And with a deep cry died.
Like a great elm on some meadow lone,
Bent in the lengthened storm with one loud
    moan—
        Is stricken to earth at last,
        By a severer blast,
Albeit clinging still the tender vine
Though long since dead; so did her arms en-
    twine
His prostrate form; so on his breast her face
Did calmly sleep, when they were found cold—cold
    in death's embrace."

        A solemn murmur stirred
The Indian group, Tiouka's tender lids
Wept generously; meanwhile Oulissi bids
His stranger-guest the tragic tale to trace
On birchen leaves, so time would not erase,
        In symbols of the tribe
        To which the unhappy bride
Belonged: as soon as Rodlyn's task was done—
Assembled all—the warrior read—fair rose the
    morning sun.

        With promise to return
An early day, Sylvalla to present
Oulissi, meanwhile, nodding free assent—

He leaves Tiouko and her Indian lord,
Heart-cheered and grateful, as, with one accord
   They pledge him their good will;
   By the near flowing rill—
By the great forest and surrounding plain—
By the Great Spirit, whom they said did reign
Over all these, and over their firesides,
Ah! surely, some religion in the red man's heart
   abides.

   The morn was well advanced
Ere Rodlyn reached his anxious wife and home;
" Oh ! wherefore leave me here so long alone?"
Sylvalla spake, and, with each hurried word
Her lips betray'd what deep commotion stirred,
   And trembling fear, her heart—
   " Thrice welcome here thou art!
Thy look again dispels the dread suspense
That filled this breast and chokèd every sense
Of feeling—save the almost hopeless hope
Of thy return; for oh! each gloomy mote
   That floated 'neath mine eye,
   And phantom that flew by
My frenzied vision, and the faintest breath,
Or sound, or slighest jar without, told but one story
   —death,"

As the grief-stricken wife
Beholds—far on the wild—wild dashing spring
Of tossing billows—each deceitful wing
That bears him not till giddy whirls the brain,
And each sound pictures to the mind again
A thousand forms—a thousand unreal fears—
And the hot orbs dry up the welling tears,
  That burst forth as the rain
  When he returns again—
So speed drops from Sylvalla's lids—hark ! hark !
  the sweet refrain.

  The morn birds sing ;
For they rejoice, and blend in with their joy,
" Sylvalla, let us these bright hours employ
In social converse, and glad tidings share
With your own Rodlyn ; drive away all care—
  Our future, spirit dear—
  No longer fraught with fear—
Nought shall disturb the happiness of our life,
For we are safe, my sweet—my darling wife :
Their hearts are ours—the red men will be brothers
  to us here."

  All tenderly she clings
Unto his side upon the grassèd lawn,
Beyond the camp; with what occurred since dawn,

In joyous strains, to listening ears, he said :
How they received him, and what pledges made,
    And every incident
    Connected with the event—
    But how her heart was stirred—
    When she the " legend " heard—
When Rodlyn told her in a whispering breath,
The story of their constancy—their suffering—and
    their death.

THE LEGEND OF "THE SCARLET DOVES."

(From the 3rd Canto of the Story of Sylvalla.)

THERE, on a mossy couch,
An Indian maid—beneath a maple bower
Awaited him, a long, long, weary hour:
    "Oh! wherefore comes he not?
    This was the chosen spot:
He pledged to meet me here ere night's moon
    past,"
Pulissa cries—while towards his tent is cast
    Her saddened, longing eye:
    "Come! come! love, or I die—
As my heart panting, almost throbs to death."
While such thoughts trembled on her lips he caught
    her, breath to breath,

    And fluttering heart to heart,
Up in his arms, and sealed the burning kiss:
"By all this love and agony of bliss

Forgive me, dearest one—
By the fair light of sun
And moon and stars, beneath whose twinkling
    beams
I do repledge my vows. In mutual dreams
    Of constant, steadfast love—
    Thou nymph-like forest dove—
Our future shall be unalloyed by fear
Or trembling doubt—come sit beside me here,
Once more I pray thee, oh ! forgive me, now,
The cruel torturing suspense I cause thee : from thy
    brow

    Dispel all shades of care,
Nor let them darken these bright orbs below,
Like those cloud shadows that the moon-beams
    Across yon gentle lake,   [throw
    But which on fleeing make
Thrice beauteous its calm face, and more fair,
As thou behold'st it now, all smiling there,
    Like as I now do thine—
    Pulissa, ever mine !
Ever ! whose love's no meteor flash, but the stars
    ' steady shine.' "

    Alas ! how darkly's stained
The brightest joy in memory's golden book,
As one by one its barèd leaves are shook

With its sin-scars of Sorrow—
Re-blighting every morrow,
And hurling down the dark pits of despair
Unburdened hearts.   See! through the cold night
   air
The moon sinks sad and low
In black clouds, far below
The western woods, and the stars quenchéd lie
Upon the breast of heaven—top the sky
The lightnings tear their ragged way—aloud the
   thunders cry.

Upon the lake and wood,
And the surrounding plain, dark shadows fall,
As weird sounds fill the air, thick as the pall
On the black form of Death :
Calm, hushed again—no breath
Felt, or a light sound heard between the loud,
Sharp rattlings of the tempest-shattered cloud :
But, hark ! a moment more,
Strange noises 'neath earth's floor ;
While echoes crowd on echoes there, as wild waves
   on the shore,
Like ocean-billows, too,
The whole land rocks, as out of the black sky
Two blood-stained doves, with wings of lightning
   fly ;

On whose self-fanned blast,
In scarlet letters cast,
Shame and Dishonour, the thick shades illume,
And pitch against young Julian's tent, when all again
  is gloom.

Six moons have passed away
Since that portentous earthquake shook the land,
While faithfully the bright and glorious band
Of true stars, night by night,
Blent with the moon their light—
Yet still he comes not, loved not as of yore—
But left, forsook, and fled for evermore ;
He heard the war-whoop, caught the battle-cry,
And followed on resolved to dare or die ;
No tidings heard of him,
Till in the shadows dim
Pulissa* sought and found him dying, sighed
Forgiveness, ere she took the draught, fell on his
  breast and died.

As her dead form was raised,
A birchen leaf, dropped from beneath her belt
(Wrapped carefully within the soft fur-felt
Of a young beaver, trim
And smooth—once worn by him,

---

* Pulissa--A Micmac Indian female name, signifying Dove.

M

When he first led his tribe on to the fight)—
His eagle-eye caught, just as he lost sight
    Of Earth, and Her, and Heaven ;
    When his heart felt the leaven
Of her all-kindling love, by Heaven sent,
To sooth, in death—wherein thus read her " death-
    song," and lament.

TO JULIAN.

Oh ! pray for me, deserted, sad and lonely—
    The only comfort thou canst now impart,
Whose late, dear love was but a fragment only
    Of that which dwelt within this shattered heart,
        Where yet thou art.

Oh ! pray for me, whose love is not the rushing
    Of riv'lets fed by melted mountain snow,
But like the streams that from the hills are gushing
    Eternally, and never cease to flow
        To vales below.

Oh ! pray for me, although thou lov'st another,
    Perchance more worthy of thy dear esteem,
For whom I feel a hope Time cannot smother,

That hers may not be, as my love hath been,
A shattered dream.

How long I've wept, how long my heart hath sighed
Is only known by my own self and thee—
Enough ! the fountains of my heart have dried,
In tearless sorrow I will bow the knee,
And pray for thee.

Oh ! pray for me, though thou didst rudely sever
The links that bound thy earliest troth to mine—
I shall love on, forever and forever !
Beyond these wilds, where 'mid the bright star-
shine,
No hearts repine.

Oh ! pray for me, while with forgiveness blending,
Shame and Dishonour fill my tortured breast—
Forsaken now, my days on earth are ending—
As sinks the sun below the clouded west,
So sinks to rest

My spirit—yet not in eternal night,
Where no sun beams, nor glows the silver moon ;
But in eternal day—more clear and bright
Than aught of earth, in fairest skies of June—
Where I'll be soon.

Oh! pray for me.   Farewell! wood, plain, and lake—
Fond parents, friends—belovèd Julian too ;
Hear my last prayer ; and now a stained soul take—
Have mercy—oh! forgive me, Manitou! ˙
          Adieu! Adieu!

          Thus, while the village slept
She wrote.   On Earth it was her last sad night,
As Cynthia shone in her full orbèd light
Upon a tear-stained page—that birchen leaf—
When finished she cried aloud for grief,
          Through long, long hours till morn;
          Wild, crazèd and forlorn,
The following day in agony she sought
The empty tent of Julian, where she caught
Sight of some arrow ·poison : In despair
She then went forth—half-naked, and with hair
          Dishevelled—on she sped
          O'er a fresh trail that led
To Julian and the battle-field. They lie, now, in one
                              [bed
          Of death : upon that tomb
Are placed his arrows, spears, and battle-bow :
Now, o'er the mound wild flowers the most loved
          grow,
          Where, every Sabbath day,
          Young couples often stray,

Repeating the sad story of their loves,
Sad fate, and legend of the blood-stained doves,
    Seen in that tempest dread!
    Since those dark hours, 'tis said,
When any woe befalls affianced bride,
Or pestilence and death stalk far and wide
Across the land, such birds, of scarlet bright,
Are sometimes seen, and sometimes heard alight
With flagging wings on Micmac tents, in the still
    hour of night.

    Sylvalla visits, too,
The lovers' grave: with her Pulissa fair
Was left an orphan, whom with tender care
She many moons had taught to read and write,
And given counsel wise to walk aright—
    That one so dear should fall
    Full long she grieved: that all
Upon her favorite and adopted child
Was lavishèd in vain—so undefiled—
    So innocent—so pure
    Pulissa seemed, full sure
She felt that young heart could not go astray:
Alas! alas! that in an evil day
His selfish love should thus despoil—thus madden!
    ruin!! slay!!!

CLASSICAL ECHOES.

BY

CHARLES PELHAM MULVANY.

—◆◆◆—

FROM THE ÆNEID OF VIRGIL.

Æneas, startled from sleep by the ghost of Hector, realizes the fact that all is lost :

MEANWHILE with manifold noise the walls of the city
    are mingled
Nearer and nearer, altho' the home of my Father
    Anchises
Stood retired from the street, and screened by shrub-
    berries round it,
The loud sounds grew clear, and the clashing of arms
    is apparent.
Out of my sleep I start, and up to the roof of the
    building,
Climb by a stair, and stand with ears that eagerly
    listen—

As, when amid the corn, a flame, by the furious
    south wind
Falls, or a rapid stream in torrent force from the
    mountain,
Floods the fields, the blooming crops and toils of the
    oxen—
Sweeping the woods in its way, and the startled
    shepherd, beholding,
Stands overwhelmed at the crash from the lofty
    cliff as hears it.

 Æneas has roused a body of Trojans to engage in resist-
ance to the victors—

Madness came with my words, then wild as a herd
    of the war-wolves
Wrapped in a cloud of the night, whose bellies
    cruelest hunger
Stings in their mad career, whose whelps in their
    dens that expect them,
Wait with dry lips at home, just so through arrows,
    through armies
Wend we to certain death, and, in the midst of the
    conflict,
Hold our way, which night with sable wings over-
          [shadows.

 The attempt to rescue Cassandra—

Lo ! by her loose hair haled, the virgin daughter of
    Priam,

See we Cassandra dragged from fane and shrine of
    Minerva,
Raising in vain appeal her ardent eyes to the
    heavens.
Only her eyes, her delicate hands the cords were
    confining.
This was a sight that Corœbus could not bear in his
    passion,
And on their midmost array he fell, determined on
    dying,
All follow on ; we charge mid foes that thicken
    around us.

    The most desperate fighting goes on around the Palace of
Priam.   Then a minute description is given of the Roman
method of storming a wall held by the enemy :

See we the gate beset by shielded stress of the
    stormers—
Ladders cling to the walls, are close prest in to the
    door posts.
Climb they on steps, their shield with left hand
    turned to the missiles.
Thus secured, with the right they grasp the battle-
    ments' summit.
Then do the Trojans in turn the towers and tops of
    the houses
Hurl on the foe, with these as they see the ruin im-
    pending

In the despair of death they seek the means of re-
sistance.
Beams adorned with gold, ancestral heir looms of
honour
Roll they down.

But Pyrrhus or Neoptolemus, son of Achilles, leads the
Greeks.

Hard by the outer porch and the very threshold is
Pyrrhus,
Proud in his bright array of weapons and glittering
armour,
As when the viper on venom fed, comes into the
sunshine
Whom in swollen sleep, cold winter long was con-
cealing,
Now having cast its skin, renewed in youth as in
beauty,
Writhing its scaly back, it rolls with crest that is lifted
High to the genial sun with three-forked tongue as
it flickers.

Then when the Palace is taken and Priam slain, comes one
of the most striking passages of the poem, in which, by the
aid of Heaven, the hero has his eyes opened to the agency of
superhuman powers of evil.

Then I look back to see what force is left to support
me.

All had gone, worn out, or with a bound from the
  ramparts
Cast their wearied limbs, or to the fires had resigned
  them.
Now I alone was left, when by the temple of Vesta,
Silently lurking hid in a secret seat for asylum,
Helen I saw—for now the flames to my wandering
  footsteps
Give bright light, as I cast my eyes on all that is
  round me—
She who the Trojans feared her foes for Troy that
  is captured,
Nor with less cause the Greeks, and wrath of the
  lord she had injured,
Hid herself there and, hated thing, sat close to the
  Altar.
Flashed the fire in my soul, and anger prompts in a
  moment
Vengeance for fatherland and fit reward for the
  guilty—
—Goes she to Sparta safe, to her native home at
  Mycenæ,
There like a Queen, to move in royal grace to a
  triumph,
Husband and home, and sons and parents there to
  revisit,
Girt with Trojan girls and Phrygian slaves to attend
  her.

Priam be slain with the sword, and Troy be sunk
    into ashes !
Shores of the Darden land be soaked with blood,
    and so often!
Never! altho' it gain scant praise to punish a
    woman,
Nor is there ought of fame to win where this is the
    conquest,
Yet shall it be my praise to have crushed the thing
    that is evil,
Giving to guilt its meed, and sating fatherland's
    ashes.

So I exclaimed, and still with maddened mind was
    borne onward—
When to my gaze, before not seen, so beautiful ever
Shone amid cloudless light my goddess mother be-
    fore me.
All-divine she seemed, and as to the dwellers in
    Heaven,
Such and so fair revealed, and with her hand as she
    held me
Stayed she my steps, as thus with roseate lips she
    addressed me :
Son! what grief can prompt in thee such measure-
    less anger,

*   *   *   *   *

No fit mark for thy hate the fatal beauty of Helen.

Blame not Paris for this; the Gods, the Gods, in
their anger

Wrought this ruin, and brought on Troy this terrible ending.

See, for I lift the veil which from the eyes of a
mortal

Hides the world unseen, and thou, refuse not obedi-
ence

Due to a mother's word, nor scorn to bend to her
bidding.

Lo! by the shattered piles, and rocks from rocks
that are rifted.

Here where the smoke uncurls with waves of dust
intermingled,

Neptune shakes the walls, and deep upheaved with
his trident

Smites foundations down, and from its centre the
city

Far and wide overthrows.   By the Scæan gate in
her anger,

Juno sits supreme, and from the ships to the foeman

Girt with the sword she calls.

    *   *   *   *   *

Said she, and shrouded her form in densest shades
of the darkness.

Terrible forms appear, and boding ill to the Trojans
Powers of the mighty Gods!

If in our Universities more stress were laid on the render-
ing the Greek and Latin authors into not merely literal, but
adequate and correct English, much more might be perma-
nently assimilated. Even to the English student, access to
an English version of Virgil, not translated into the manner
of Pope, nor of Chaucer, nor of Scott, but aiming to repro-
duce the rythm of the original, and as far as possible the
spirit and flow of the original words, will give some flavour
of that old wine of the world's culture, of which those who
have drank deepest of the new, will avow that "the old is
better."

FROM HOMER'S ILIAD.

THE MUSE IS INVOKED.

GODDESS! declare the wrath of the son of Peleus,
　　Achilles!
Working woe, which smote with many a curse the
　　Achaians;
Many the souls of the brave it sent untimely to
　　Hades—
Souls of the heroes,—whose bodies it gave to dogs
　　for a portion,
And to the birds of the air! but the will of Zeus
　　was fulfilling,

Even from the time when first these twain were
  parted in anger—
Atreus' son—the king of men—and noble Achilles.
  Which was it, say, of the gods, that impelled
  them striving together ?
Son was he of Leto and Zeus? for he being angered,
Sent on the host a deadly plague, and the people
  were dying,
For that Atreus' son had done despite to his prophet
Chryses ; for he had come where lay the ships of
  Achaia,
Willing to ransom his child, and bearing gifts that
  were priceless :
And in his hand he held the wreaths of far-darting
  Apollo
High on a golden wand, and he spake to all the
  Achaians,
But to the two Atridæ first, the chiefs of the
  people !
'Atreus' sons and others, the mail-clad men of
  Achaia,
So may the gods bestow, in the homes of Olympus
  abiding,
Capture of Priam's city, and safe return to your
  home-land ;
Only loose ye my child from bonds, and take ye the
  ransom,

Fearing the son of Zeus the king, far-darting Apollo.'
So the old man spake, but the other Achaians
applauded,
Willing to loose the maid and take the generous
ransom.
But not so did it please the king of men—
Agamemnon,
For he dismissed him in scorn, and hard was the
word that he added :
" Not again old man, at the hollow ships let me find
thee
Either delaying now, or afterward hither returning,
Lest there avail thee not the staff of the god or his
garland;
Her I will not release, till that old age come upon
her
There, in my house at Argos, far away from her
country.
Go ! and incense me not, that so thy return be the
safer."
So he said, but the old man feared his word, and
obeyed him.
Silent he went on his way by the shore of the clan-
gorous ocean ;
Then, as he went apart, with many a prayer he en-
treated
King Apollo, the god, conceived of fair haired Leto,

THE PROPHET CALCHAS DECLARES THE REASON
OF APOLLO'S ANGER. .

Then taking courage spake to them the excellent
    Prophet:
" Not for vow unpaid is his wroth nor hecatomb
    stinted,
But for his Priest, whom late the king Agememnon
    insulted ;
Neither releasing his child, nor yet accepting the
    ransom ;
Therefore gives the Far-darter griefs and still will
    he give them ;
Nor will withhold from the plague his heavy hands
    in his anger,
Till that the bright eyed maid be sent again to her
    father—
Sent without ransom or price, and a sacred hecatomb
    offered
There at Chrysa's shrine, and thus alone can we
    please him."
He having spoken thus thereon sat down, but among
    them
Rose the hero Atrides, King of men, Agamemnon,
Full of rage, in his heart the black blood worked in
    his fury,
Waxing fierce, and his eyes were like to coals that
    are kindled.
    N

Calchas, first, with look of bitter wrath, he accosted—
" Prophet of evil, never yet good tidings thou bring-
        est,—
Ever it glads thy heart to speak a message of mis-
        chief."

ACHILLES REJOINS.

" Ah me, sordid soul, with impudence clad as a gar-
        ment,
How shall any obey thy word of all the Achaians !
Either to march on the way, or bravely fight with
        the foeman.
I came not aggrieved in aught by the warrior Tro-
        jans,
Hither to fight, since they to me in nought have
        offended.
Never in hostile raid have they driven my oxen or
        horses ;
Nor in the fertile fields of far off populous Phthia,
Have they the crops destroyed, for far and wide
        intervene there
Shadowy mountain heights, and sounding billows
        between us :
But for pleasure of thine, Oh, shameless one, have
        we followed,
Fighting in feud of thy brother and thee,—oh, thou
        that art dog-faced."

TRANSLATIONS FROM HORACE.

Ode I. XI.

Nay, love ! seek not to know that which the gods,
  hiding from me, from thee,
Term of life have assigned, Leuconöe, this thou
  shalt not foresee—
Better were it to bear evil or good, all that the fates
  ordain,
Be this tempest the last, or if the storm Jupiter
  sends again—
Storm that frets with its foam rocks that oppose
  ever the Tuscan wave.
Be thou wise, and the wine pour for my lips,—hope
  not against the grave ;
Hope not! even as we speak, envious time fleets on
  his wings away,—
Now the Present enjoy, and if you can, trust not
  the Future day.

Toronto, May 3, 1880.

Ode I. II.

Snow-storms enough, on earth, and dreadful hail-
  stones
Hath the sire sent, and with his right hand reddened,

Hurling his vengeful thunderbolts at temples,
      Frighted the city—

Frighted the nations lest that the disastrous
Age should return of Pyrrha, and the portents,
When the whole herd of Proteus from the sea-beach
      Climbed to the hill-tops,

So that the fishes swam around the elm-tree
Where in the branches late the wood-doves nestled,
And in dismay the gentle deer were floating,
      'Whelmed in the deluge.

We have beheld the yellow tide of Tiber,
Thrust from the Tuscan bank that checked his onset,
Rush to throw down the monuments of Numa—
      Temples of Vesta.

While to the plaint of Ilia too attentive,
Comes he her champion, from his left bank rushing,
Prompt at her prayer, which Jupiter approves not,
      He in his anger !

Yet shall our youth made few by these dissensions,
Hear of the sword our citizens have sharpened,—
Sword for our Persian foes were better fitted—
      And of the battles.

Whom of the gods shall now the people pray to,
Now in our need ; and say with what entreaty

Shall in their hymns the consecrated maidens
      Sing to their Vesta !

Say to what god shall Jupiter apportion
Task of atonement ! come at length we pray thee,
Veiling in cloud the glory of thy shoulders,—
      Augur Apollo !

Or if thou rather, smiling one of Eryx,
Over whom Mirth and Love so lightly hover—
Or of thy slighted race and thy descendants,
      Father, bethink thee.

Thou that with sport all too prolonged art sated,
Who in war's shout and polished arms delightest,
And the stern soldier's face, in battle looking
      Fierce on the foeman.

TO LYDIA.

ODE I. XXV.

SELDOMER now the wanton youths thy windows
Smite with rude summons of their blows, quick
    tapping,
Nor do they break thy sleep ; and now the door
    clings
        Close to the doorway

Which was of old so ready to be moving
On the smooth hinge, and less and less thou hearest,—
"Can'st thou, while I through the long night am
    dying,
                    Lydia, slumber?"

Now in old age to lovers grown disdainful,
Lone in some alley vainly thou art weeping,
While by the waning moon the Thracian wind blows
                    Wilder and wilder.

While fierce desire and passion that surpasses
That which is wont to chafe the dams of horses,
Rages around your heart to madness driven,
                    Bitterly rueing

That the glad youth takes pleasure in the freshness
Of the green ivy and the myrtle blossom,
Throws the dry leaves and withered where the
    Winter
                    Mates with the East wind.

ODE I. XXIII.

JUST as wild as a fawn—Chloe you fly from me—
Which through mountainous wilds seeks where its
    mother is—

Scared and not without idle
Fear of wind-shaken aspen leaves.

If with tremulous boughs something that passes there
Moves the quivering brake, lizards that flit through it
    Stir the leaves of the hedges,—
    Knees and heart they are failing thee!

Yet pursue I not thee, fierce as a tiger is,
Or some lion that roars; eager to mangle you!
    Cease to follow your mother,
    Flower full ripe for love's gathering!

TORONTO, May 7, 1880.

EPODE XV.

CALM in the summer night, the moon unclouded was
    Amid the stars of lesser light,   [shining
When to the gods above, despite and falsehood de-
    signing,
    With me you swore great oaths of might.

Close as the ivy clings to the guardian oak, you
    were clinging,   .
    With languid arms around me twined,
Swearing, while wolves hunt sheep, while storms
    Orion is bringing,

While sweeps the wave the winter wind—
While in the breeze flow loose Apollo's odorous
    tresses,—
You swore that this our love should last—
You on whom yet my pride shall visit many
    distresses,
    If my firm purpose holdeth fast;

Deeming it not to be borne that you give your love
    to another,
    A love more just I seek with speed !
Never my firm resolve shall change, if some day or
I feel a pang too deep indeed.   [other

You, too, whoever you are—my victor now in the
    battle,
    At my defeat who strut so bold,
Rich though you be in farms and all abundance of
    cattle,
    Though thine, Pactolus flows with gold—

Though like Pythagorus sage, both wealth and wis-
    dom asserting—
    Like Nireus though your beauty glow—
She cannot possibly stop her inveterate habit of
    flirting;
    And I shall laugh—"I told you so !"
May 7, 1880.

THE HYMN TO APHRODITE—THEOCRITUS.

See Mr. Mathew Arnold's "Critical Essays." Gorgo and Praxinöe, two Syracusan ladies, visit the palace of King Ptolemy at Alexandria, to witness a grand choral service in honour of the Goddess Aphrodite. The images of Aphrodite and of her lover Adonis are displayed on silver couches. A celebrated singer renders the Hymn.

GORGO.

Is Praxinöe in ?

PRAXINÖE.

Come in, my dearest Gorgo !
Why, what a time since you called! Get a chair,
please Eunöe, quickly.
See for a cushion.

GORGO.

'Tis well, 'tis well.

PRAXINÖE.

Sit down, I beseech you.

GORGO.

O what a risk—it is all but a chance I got hither in
safety,
Such was the crowd, Praxinöe,—such the throng of
the horses.

Everywhere booted men and guards in tunics of
scarlet!
Not to be passed is the street—and you, who live at
a distance!

PRAXINÖE.

It is my husband's fault; on this remote place insist-
ing,
Just to prevent us two from neighbourly living together,—
All for spite.

* * * * * * * *

GORGO.

Come, let us go to the service at Ptolemy's royal
palace,
Held in prayer to Adonis—the Queen's decorations
are lovely.

PRAXINÖE.

You have well and sensibly spoken;
Get me my mantle quick, my sun-shade bring. I
shall need it.
No! child, you shall not come! there's a big bear
bites little boys there—
Horses who kick! Well, cry if you like, better that
than be crippled.

Well, let us go,   Stay Phrygia, call the little one
  indoors,
Shut the dog within and close the door to all comers.
O ye gods, what a crowd !

*   *   *   *   *   *   *   *

GORGO [*within the palace.*]

Hush, Praxinöe! see that clever singer from Argos,
She is about to begin to chant the hymn to the goddess !
She who last year at the dirge was held the best of
  the singers,
Sure she will sing worth hearing—and see ! she be-
  gins already.

THE HYMN TO APHRODITE.

Lady !   Who lovest the heights of Golgi's hill and
  of Ida,
And the Erycian steep, whose toys are gold, Aphrodite,
How have the light-footed Hours, from Acheron
  ceaselessly flowing,
Now in a twelve-month's time brought back to thee
  thy Adonis !
Slowest of all the gods the dear Hours come, but a
  welcome

Greeteth them still, for still to all some gift they are
    bringing.

Cypris! Dione's child, from a mortal thou an im-
    mortal,

As is the story with men, hast made the Queen
    Berenice!

Thou on the earth-born breast divine ambrosia drop-
    ping.

Therefore, O thou of numerous names and numerous
    temples,

Queen Berenice's child, Arsinöe, lovely as Helen,

Grateful greets with gifts of all good things thy
    Adonis.

There are spread all fruits that grow on trees of the
    forest,

There the green lettuce is piled, secure in baskets of
    silver,

Perfume of Syrian myrrh there fills the gold alabas-
    ters;

There all cakes are spread, by women wrought at the
    meal-board;

Every kind of flour with snow-white meal inter-
    mingled;

All that sweet honey blends with faultless oil of the
    olive.

There all fowls of the air, and creeping things have
    been offered.

O, the ebony ! O, the gold and the ivory carving,
Lo ! where the eagle soars, to Zeus his cup-bearer
    bringing,
Softer than sleep are there the purple coverlets
    hanging :
So will Miletus say, and so the shepherd of Samos.
Lo ! two couches are spread, the one for lovely
    Adonis,
One for Cypris herself and one for rosy Adonis ;
He will not hurt with his kiss, whose lips in youth
    are unbearded,
He who at eighteen years or nineteen years is a
    bridegroom !
Cypris ! now farewell ! alone with thy lover we leave
    thee,
But with the morning's dawn we shall go down to
    the seaboard,   .
And with loose hair and robes, with besoms bare we
    shall sing thee.
Welcome thou comest, Adonis, here, and to Acheron
    also,
Sole of the demigods thou, for this not King Agamem-
    non,
Gained, nor Ajax himself, the great though trucu-
    lent hero—
Nor brave Hector, the eldest of Hecuba's hundred
    children,

Nor Patroclus nor Pyrrhus from Troy returned to
    his homeland.
Be propitious, Adonis dear, to our crops give a bless-
    ing—
Dear thou comest, Adonis, and dear wilt thou be in
    returning.

GORGO.

Well Praxinöe! sure the girl is remarkably clever,
Blest to know so much, thrice blest to sing it so
    sweetly;
But let us go—without dinner is still my man Dio-
    cleides;
Always cross, when hungry his temper is perfectly
    savage—
Dear Adonis, farewell, and may you return to us
    happy.

INDEX.